SLEEPLESS

Also by Thomas Fahy

THE UNSPOKEN

SLEEPLESS

THOMAS FAHY

Simon & Schuster Books for Young Readers
New York London Toronto Sydney

SIMON & SCHUSTER BOOKS FOR YOUNG READERS
An imprint of Simon & Schuster Children's Publishing Division
1230 Avenue of the Americas, New York, New York 10020

This book is a work of fiction. Any references to historical events, real people, or real locales are used fictitiously. Other names, characters, places, and incidents are products of the author's imagination, and any resemblance to actual events or locales or persons, living or dead, is entirely coincidental.

Book design by Lucy Ruth Cummins
The text for this book is set in Caslon.
Manufactured in the United States of America
10 9 8 7 6 5 4 3 2 1
Library of Congress Cataloging-in-Publication Data
Fahy, Thomas Richard.
Sleepless / Thomas Fahy.—1st ed.
p. cm.
Summary: Terrified by the gruesome nightmares and unexplained bouts of sleepwalking that seem to be affecting her and many other students at Saint Opportuna High, Emma and her friends become even more unnerved when, after several deaths, they begin to suspect that something is causing them to kill in their sleep.
ISBN 978-1-4169-5901-4 (hardcover)
ISBN 978-1-4169-9638-5 (eBook)
[1. Sleep disorders—Fiction. 2. Murder—Fiction. 3. Horror stories.] I. Title.
PZ7.F14317Sle 2009 [Fic]—dc22
2008007310

IN LOVING MEMORY OF
MY GRANDPARENTS

ELEANOR ELIZABETH FAHY
(FEBRUARY 14, 1918—JULY 27, 2002)

THOMAS PATRICK FAHY
(AUGUST 13, 1918—AUGUST 5, 1994)

RICHARD DANIEL MCCARTHY
(JUNE 6, 1917—JUNE 11, 2001)

ROSE ANNE MCCARTHY
(JULY 4, 1919—FEBRUARY 10, 1996)

ACKNOWLEDGMENTS

Once again I am so grateful to David Gale, the staff at Simon & Schuster, Elaine Markson, and everyone at the Markson Agency. I also have several friends whose unfailing support is staggering: Daniel Kurtzman, who helped shape this project from the beginning and who continually challenges me to be a better writer; Laura Garrett, whom I rely on time and time again for insight into the teenage mind; and Susann Cokal, whose writing and artistry continue to inspire me. I am grateful for all of your expertise, fictional input, encouragement, and, of course, friendship.

Lastly, I want to thank my loving family for everything else—particularly Tom and Eileen Fahy, Mike and Jen, and my nieces Tommi-Rose and Ellie Lynn.

CONTENTS

PROLOGUE

Emma doesn't really notice the cold night air or the damp grass beneath her feet. Only the howling sound in her ears. That same sound dragged her out of bed a while ago. It made her walk downstairs and go outside to the shed where her dad keeps the old splintery shovel. That sound is the reason she has to keep digging—to find out what it wants.

Her arms move up and down fast. The scoop of the shovel bites into the brittle earth, and the muscles in her lower back burn. Dirt is piling up next to her. Some of it has even started to spill back into the ground.

"Em?"

The voice is barely audible above the howling. She doesn't answer. She's too afraid to speak. Then something grabs her. It claws into each arm before spinning her around.

"What are you doing?" the figure in front of her asks.

"I have to find him," she says flatly.

"Who?"

The kitchen door slams suddenly, and the noise wakes Emma from her trance. She stands there, looking first at the surprise on her father's face and then over at her little sister, Gwen, who is standing in the doorway. The yellow-white light from inside makes her sister's nightgown glow.

"Go back to bed," Dad calls out to Gwen. He puts his arm around Emma's shoulders.

He leads her inside the house and up the stairs, carefully—just the way he used to help Mom when she was sick for all those months, Emma remembers.

"She's sleepwalking . . . like the others," her dad whispers to his friend Dr. Feldman the next morning. They're sitting in the living room as Emma stands on the staircase—out of sight but close enough to hear. Besides, her father is the worst whisperer in the world. He tries so hard to sound quiet that his voice just gets louder. The doctor wonders if their next-door neighbor, Ms. Martinique Dupré, is to blame. Everyone in town knows that she practices "the voodoo," though no one has actually seen her do it. Like Emma and Gwen and Dad, Ms. Dupré moved to Sea Cliff from the South. She lived in New Orleans until Katrina.

Emma thinks Ms. Dupré is okay; she doesn't care one iota—as her dad likes to say—if the woman practices voodoo or plays the accordion, which Emma considers the worst-sounding instrument ever invented. Still, Ms. Dupré's place does smell like incense when you walk by, and that can make folks wonder. It sure doesn't stop people from visiting her to have their fortunes told, though.

"Do you think your daughter is depressed?" Dr. Feldman asks, and Mr. Montgomery answers without his whispering voice.

"She lost her mother fourteen months ago, Jack. But that doesn't mean she's fixing to hurt herself . . . or somebody else."

Dr. Feldman doesn't say anything for a while. When he finally speaks, his voice is too soft to hear, as if he knows someone might be listening. His words run together faster now, and Emma can't concentrate anymore. She hurries downstairs and into the kitchen. The room feels hot. Her forehead is damp with sweat, and she wonders if the oven is on. No. They hardly cook anymore. Not without Mom around.

Emma bumps into the table, tipping over the chair. She feels dizzy and off balance. *This can't be happening to me,* she tells herself. She doesn't want to end up like Selene, like those other students at Saint Opportuna High. All of a sudden Emma wishes her mom were here right now. She would know what to do.

Emma hurries outside.

A cool, playful wind whips past the oak tree in the middle of the backyard. Orange-red leaves cling to the tree branches, and they shake nervously with every gust. Emma steps over to the place where she was digging last night and notices the upturned soil. Dad must have filled the hole sometime this morning, she figures. The brown, rectangular patch looks like a Band-Aid.

Her stomach knots. Something about the filled-in hole makes her uneasy. Emma gets down on her knees and grabs a handful of dirt. It feels moist and thick and heavy. Then she puts her ear against the ground. She doesn't want to, but she can't stop herself. She has to know something.

Emma presses the side of her face harder against the ground. There seems to be a murmur somewhere beneath her. She closes her eyes to concentrate, but the wind just gets louder in her ears.

Emma pushes herself away from the spot and gets to her feet. She takes a few steps back toward the house and turns—

A set of piercing black eyes hovers right in front of her. Staring. *A ghost,* Emma thinks, as her body stiffens. She struggles to breathe.

No, she realizes. It's not a ghost at all. It's Ms. Dupré, standing on the back porch of her house and looking over the short row of hedges that separates their yards. Some kind of gray paste covers the old woman's face, and her body is cloaked in a gown of deep purple. She isn't watching Emma, though. She seems to be looking through her, looking at something much farther away.

The wind kicks up again, and Emma turns back to the spot where she was digging. Something terrible is about to happen, she realizes. In truth she knew it as soon as the howling sounds began. She knew it as soon as Dad found her in the backyard last night. Just like she knows it now.

Someone else will die soon, she tells herself. *Someone else will die, and I'll be responsible.* A few days after the first time you walk in your sleep, you kill someone.

That's how the end begins.

WEDNESDAY

SIX DAYS EARLIER . . .

1
SMOKE AND MIRRORS

Jake Hardale likes old cars. Everything about them. The grease that gets under his fingernails after replacing an alternator or changing the oil. The smell of a warm V-8 engine. The hum of tires against the asphalt. That's why he likes his part-time job at Island Auto Repair so much. He can turn on his iPod and block everything out except the car he's working on.

He likes his job more than school, that's for sure. But Saint Opportuna High isn't the worst place in the world. Some of the girls are hot. Especially Emma Montgomery. Sure, she's a total nerd, always studying and carrying around a book, but still, she's hot. Besides, she's nothing like those pretentious theater chicks and the cheerleaders with their plastic smiles and stadium-sized attitudes. No, Jake prefers Emma, with her long legs and crooked smile.

The art history teacher, Dr. Silas Beecher, is one of the other okay things about Saint Opportuna. For starters, the paintings in his class look totally wild when you're baked. Also, Dr. Beecher invited Jake to be part of a "secret" society after their trip to New Orleans—when he took Jake and Emma and several other students to the Lower Ninth Ward to help build houses there this summer. Well, the meetings aren't actually secret, Jake admits, but they all promised to keep quiet about what happened in New Orleans. That makes them feel secretive.

Sure, he has never been one for clubs and cliques and that sort of thing, but it felt good to be asked. Besides, the trip was for their senior project, and they have to put together a slide show and write an essay for college credit. Dr. Beecher has offered to help them.

That art class and this secret society are the only things Jake has ever given a damn about in high school. Well, those things and Emma. And the English class where he's reading Hemingway's *The Sun Also Rises.* He likes the way those characters talk.

Sometimes, being around the other people who went to New Orleans makes him feel rotten inside about what happened, but Jake needs them too. They were there. They all made the same promise.

When he starts thinking too much about that trip, Jake can always turn to his job at Island Auto. That makes him feel good. He has brought in more business than any other employee. Even his boss, Hiram Nichols, who mostly communicates in wheezes and grunts, says every once in a while, "You're a damn popular mechanic."

You bet your incredibly large ass I am, Jake imagines saying but never does. For all the money he brings in, he ought to be promoted to manager or something. But as long as Hiram doesn't ask too many questions, Jake is fine with the way things are.

Maybe Hiram doesn't care why most of the students at Saint Opportuna bring their cars to his shop for everything from oil changes and state inspections to fender benders. Maybe he hasn't noticed that the alley behind the garage always smells like a bong. Or maybe he just doesn't know that Island Auto is the best place to buy weed in Sea Cliff and that Jake Hardale is the most popular dealer in town. Almost everyone comes to Jake: cheerleaders, basketball players, dorks in the chess club, and even Mr. Yankovich, the gym teacher who is missing half of his right index finger.

Jake glances down the main road. He has often wondered if Sea Cliff is the smallest town in the world or if it just feels that way. It's gotta be one of the smallest on Long Island, he thinks. It's only one square mile, and the "downtown" is four blocks long. Most people can walk it in about as much time as it takes to sneeze. On one side of the auto shop is a dingy Irish pub, and on the other is Mystic Dreams—a store that must have opened in the 1960s and never realized that the 1960s ended. Inside, you can buy crystals, beads, Zen alarm clocks, incense, self-help books, futons, statues of Buddha, pipes, and, of course, Birkenstocks. You can also make an appointment to have your fortune told by Ms. Martinique Dupré.

Sure, for a while he figured Ms. Dupré was just a quack, a scam artist with a southern accent. But after spending a month in New Orleans he thinks there might be something to magic and spells after all. That's why he's on his way to her now. For almost a week he has been planning to get his fortune told—ever since he stopped wanting to dream. These days nothing helps him clear his head. Smoking out. Surfing the Net. Listening to music. He just can't stop seeing things when his eyes close. Terrible things—wake-up-with-the-sweats terrible. Himself gasping for air. Swallowing mouthfuls of black liquid. That half-buried hand with its stiff, curled fingers.

Terrible things that all started in New Orleans . . .

Jake doesn't remember dreaming, just the feeling of something dripping steadily on his face. Something thick and sticky. That's why he opened his eyes. At first all he could see was the bright New Orleans moon pouring through the windows of the half-built house.

Selene Johnson stood above him, wearing a white nightgown that fell to her ankles. She was twelve or thirteen years old. The knife in her left hand pointed toward his forehead, and the blade was dark with blood. As his eyes started to adjust, he could see blood smeared on her nightgown, too. It seemed to be all over her body. That was what was dripping on his head, he realized. Blood from the knife.

Jake backed away with a start and grabbed Caitlin Harris's arm. She had been asleep next to him, Jake in his Jockey shorts and Caitlin in nothing more than a loose T-shirt. They stared at Selene and the knife.

"What the hell?" Jake blurted out, his voice cracking slightly.

Selene didn't say a word. She blinked a few times and turned around, walking with heavy steps toward the front door.

"Selene?" Caitlin asked, but the girl kept going. Caitlin turned to Jake. "Come on!"

"What?"

She had pulled on a pair of jeans before Jake even stood up. "We have to find out what happened."

Jake's body ached all over as he got dressed and followed Caitlin out the door. He thought he was used to his sleeping bag, and to the hard surface of the newly laid floors. But his stiff neck and shoulders said otherwise. Because of Caitlin, he didn't really care. She had never paid much attention to him at school, but during their first night in New Orleans they'd smoked one of his joints and made out in the church basement. He couldn't believe that someone so beautiful—with her blond hair and blue eyes and muscular-thin body—would be attracted to him. But everyone gets lucky once in a while, he figured.

Habitat for Humanity was building several houses in the Lower Ninth Ward, and fifteen students and three teachers from Saint Opportuna had signed up to help for the month of August. For most people the phrase "signed up" implies something voluntary. For Jake, Principal Mackey had a different idea: "Do this, and you can stay another semester on academic probation. But this is your last chance, Mr. Hardale. Got it?"

So that's how Jake had volunteered. He had never been to a place as thickly hot as New Orleans. Nighttime didn't make things cooler; it just made you wish things were cooler. A mean trick, Jake thought. During the day they worked nonstop—putting up walls, laying floors, installing plumbing. After sunset the students were supposed to sleep on cots in the basement of Reverend Michaels's church. The girls in one room. The boys in the other. But Jake and Caitlin had been sneaking out every night and staying in the house they were building.

Neither of them spoke as they followed Selene outside and up the narrow street. Blood still dripped from the knife every so often, leaving a trail on the dirt and broken stone. They passed the skeletal frames of several unfinished houses and entered the older part of the neighborhood. Fallen trees. Abandoned cars. Homes half collapsed. Rotted-out furniture. Telephone poles too exhausted to stand up straight. Debris was still everywhere, as if the hurricane had just come and gone.

Selene paused in front of Reverend Michaels's church. It was one of the few buildings standing. The red wooden slats looked blue in the moonlight, and the iron cross at the high point of the roof tilted forward. Selene stepped into the front courtyard and followed one of the paths around the side.

The back of the church was a graveyard—one of the countless graveyards where bodies had risen out of their tombs and been washed away in the waters of Katrina and the flood that followed. Now the headstones were mostly restored. Some of the bodies had been reburied. Others had never been found.

Selene stood perfectly still by a stone statue of an angel with a sword. They both stared down at a new plot.

Caitlin and Jake approached slowly. The hole wasn't as deep as Jake expected. A few feet, nothing more, and the dirt at the bottom appeared lumpy and uneven. Jake heard Caitlin fumbling for the key chain in her pocket, and then she pulled out the small light attached to it.

She flashed the beam into the pit, and it reflected off something silver—a watch. Reverend Michaels's silver watch.

Jake recognized it right away. The thing was way too big for the reverend's thin wrist, and it was always sliding up and down his arm when he talked—which he liked to do a lot. Caitlin's light caught its surface again, and that's when Jake noticed the dark, curled fingers. Hard, frozen. Jake grabbed Caitlin's wrist and moved the light toward the head of the grave. It stopped on Reverend Michaels's half-buried face. Blood still seeped out of a gash that ran from his left eye to his chin.

Caitlin gasped and dropped the light. . . .

Now, back in Sea Cliff, Jake realizes that something strange is happening to him. Something that he suspects has to do with that night, so he figures his appointment to get his fortune told can't hurt.

The wind tosses leaves down Main Street carelessly, and each gust sounds like a wave crashing against the shore. He considers taking a hit from the reefer in his pocket, but he doesn't want to be late. There'll be plenty of time for that after work, he reminds himself.

Jake doesn't know what to expect when he arrives. The front of the store is empty. As usual. Sometimes Mr. Offutt, the proprietor, sits behind the register, but today he's not there. A sign on the counter near the entry reads

READINGS BY MADEMOISELLE DUPRÉ

IN BACK ⟶

Jake steps into a narrow hallway. A small mirror hangs on the wall, and he pauses in front of his reflection. His face seems pitted, as if parts of it are missing. He touches the glass and realizes that the silvering has gone bad. Bits of gray and black appear in the reflection.

After Jake passes through a curtain of red, blue, and purple beads, he sees Ms. Dupré sitting behind a desk. Her colorful gowns make her stand out in Sea Cliff, that's for sure, and today she wears a flowing crimson shawl. The purplish-blue walls match the color of the building's exterior, and stacks of books crowd the room. Some of them lie horizontally on shelves, but most are just piled on the floor—old, yellowing, well worn. A strong aroma of incense fills the air. On one side of the desk two candles burn. A tarot deck sits in the center. It looks older than the books, Jake thinks. Much older.

"Mr. Hardale." Ms. Dupré's voice is slow and easy, as if her words aren't in a hurry to get anywhere. "Please. Sit."

As soon as Jake drops into the chair across from her, she reaches for his hands. Her wrinkled fingers trace the lines on his palms, and his eyes feel heavy watching her movements.

"Mix the deck with your left. Like this." She lets go of him and makes a counterclockwise motion above the cards with her hand.

Jake starts to spread the deck in circles. He notices a design on the back of each card: a small red eye. He continues to swirl the cards around on the table, watching them fan out and twist together in new combinations. Dozens of eyes are staring up at him now.

Jake wishes he had gotten high after all.

"Stack them with both hands," Ms. Dupré says with an encouraging nod. "Good. Now, cut the deck with your left."

When he finishes, Jake looks up and sees the candlelight flickering in her amber eyes. The cards move quickly, naturally in her hands. She lays six of them on the table, facedown. They form a cross.

She turns over the first: the Ten of Swords. The card shows a man's body on the ground—swords impaling his back and blood pooling alongside him.

Without speaking, she moves onto the next one: the Hanged Man. Here an elderly man is being crucified upside down. His limbs are wiry, too weak to pull free. His face twists in pain.

The Devil appears on the next card. Fire rages behind his greenish skin and fanglike teeth. He points down at the rocky ground beneath him, as if asking the viewer to kneel.

The Eight of Swords follows. On this card a woman has

been blindfolded and bound to a stake. Eight sharp, blood-stained swords have been thrust into the ground, forming a circle around her.

Ms. Dupré pauses before turning over the fifth card: the Wheel of Fortune. A man with a long white beard has fallen on his hands and knees. He struggles to hold up a heavy bronze wheel on his back. In its center rests a blindfolded angel with golden wings.

"You must go," Ms. Dupré announces. The easiness in her voice has dried up. She leans back in her chair as if she's trying to get away from him. But whether she's afraid for herself or for him, Jake can't tell.

"What the hell? You haven't told me what any of this means," Jake protests.

Ms. Dupré's face tightens, and he can see creases in the skin around her eyes and lips. "A new beginning is underway for you."

"Cool," he says with relief. "Like a promotion?"

"There is something inside of you, Mr. Hardale. Something dangerous and sharp, like the edge of a knife." She stops speaking, and the flames no longer appear in her eyes.

Jake stands up, unable to speak at first.

"As far as fortunes go," he begins, his voice unsteady, "this one totally sucks!"

Ms. Dupré doesn't say anything, so Jake continues: "What about this card? You didn't even turn it over."

"Don't—" Ms. Dupré reaches for it, but Jake is too fast. He lifts it close to his face. The red eyes of Death—eyes like those on the back of every card—look directly at him. He is riding a horse along a dusty road, and a black cloak covers most of his bony frame.

"Is this supposed to scare me?" Jake asks angrily, tossing the card on the table. "Huh?"

Ms. Dupré remains silent and still.

"You're such a"—he struggles for the word—"cliché!"

He knows he could have come up with something better if he'd had more time, but he can't think straight. Not right now. He needs to get out of there.

He pushes his way back through the beads—past the stained mirror and the feng shui books and the cheap meditation fountains. He pushes his way through the empty store and goes outside—where the wind is less urgent now and the sun seems bright after the bluish shadows of Mystic Dreams.

Why would anyone spend money to hear that kind of crap? Jake wonders. Come to think of it, he forgot to pay. Good. If he wanted to feel like hell, he could do that without spending a dime. Getting up before noon on a Saturday. Doing homework. Acknowledging his parents' disappointment in him.

There are plenty of ways to be miserable in this world, that's for sure.

"Hi, Jake," someone calls out.

Jake looks up and sees Emma Montgomery standing in front of Island Auto.

"Hey," he says, still distracted but happy to see her. He watches her in Dr. Beecher's class all the time. Jake knows the angle of her head when she takes notes and the fluttering sound of her voice when she laughs. He knows what her fingers look like when they play imaginary piano keys on her desk. He even knows that she likes to slip off her right shoe as soon as she sits down. Sometimes they talk after class. Twice they've sat together on Dr. Beecher's couch at the meetings for the secret society. But Emma doesn't smoke out, so she never comes to the shop. *This is her first time here,* Jake thinks with a smile. He likes having her around. He likes the way her black skirt and stockings make her legs look.

"So?" Emma asks.

"What?"

"You told me to come by after school. You said you had something for me."

"Oh, yeah." Jake nods. While Ms. Dupré was giving him the worst fortune ever, he forgot about the gift he bought Emma. He was in Greenwich Village last weekend and stopped in a used bookstore near Union Square. Jake didn't know what he wanted until he saw a shelf filled with books by Hemingway. They looked and smelled old, but in a good way. Crisp yellow pages. The faint odor of cigarettes. He found a hardbound copy of *The Sun Also Rises* from the 1950s.

"I left it in the office. Hold on a sec," Jake says.

He hurries inside to the mostly empty file cabinet, which is next to the sink and the mini-fridge. In the bottom drawer Jake finds the brown bag with the note he wrote on it:

JAKE HARDALE'S PROPERTY
DO NOT TOUCH

Jake takes the book out of the bag carefully and looks at it again. The reddish cover has slight water damage in the lower right corner, but otherwise it's in good condition. He opens to the title page. Maybe he should write an inscription, Jake thinks. Even something simple like "From Jake." But for some reason he thinks she'll like the book better if it isn't marked.

Jake looks up and catches his reflection in the small mirror above the sink. His face isn't distorted here, but the paleness of his skin bothers him today. It reminds him of his father's face.

Jake hurries outside.

Emma is leaning against a sky-blue Dodge Dart that needs new brake pads.

"Here," Jake says, holding out the book. "It's for you."

She takes the book and feels the cover with her fingertips before opening it. Her green-brown eyes widen in surprise.

"What?" Jake asks.

"You're the last guy I'd expect to get a book from, that's all."

"Why?"

"I don't know," she says, hooking some of her long brown hair behind her right ear. "I didn't think you cared about this stuff."

"I like Hemingway." Jake glances down at his feet. "And I knew you could understand that."

Emma smiles. Then she turns a few pages and reads: "'You are all a lost generation.'"

Jake likes watching the way the small birthmark on her right cheek gets darker when she concentrates on something. "I thought you'd like it."

Emma looks up from the page. "I do."

Right then a 1967 Pontiac Firebird convertible with leopard-skin seat covers pulls into the driveway of Island Auto. It's Jeremy Carson. Outside of Dr. Beecher's class Jake sees Jeremy only here. He isn't one of Jake's frequent-flyers, but every few weeks he comes in for an ounce or two.

"Hey," Jeremy calls out to both of them, still sitting behind the wheel. "This engine is smoking more than you do."

Steam pushes its way through the front grille, and Jake realizes that Jeremy is here with legitimate car problems today.

"Pull into the garage and turn off the engine," Jake tells him before facing Emma again. He's annoyed by Jeremy's crack, but that's not it, really. He's annoyed because of that damn fortuneteller, because he can't get her words out of his head:

There is something inside of you, Mr. Hardale. Something dangerous and sharp, like the edge of a knife.

"I guess I should go," Emma says, glancing down at the book and smiling again. "Thanks."

"Sure."

Emma hesitates. "Is everything okay?"

"I feel pretty rotten," Jake admits, liking the sound of Hemingway's words on his tongue.

"Why?"

"Just tired. I haven't been sleeping well." Jake stuffs his hands in his pockets and glances down at the book in her hands. Her fingers are moving slightly against the cover. "You know Ms. Dupré, right?" Jake asks.

"A little," Emma says. "She's my neighbor."

"Do you think she's the real thing?"

"What do you mean?"

Jake shrugs. "I don't know. Forget it . . . I'd better see to Jeremy's car."

She stares at him for a moment, as if she's trying to decide whether or not to push him for an answer. "Okay," she says with hesitation. "Thanks for the book."

Jake watches Emma walk past Mystic Dreams toward the end of the downtown, where Memorial Park overlooks the choppy waters of Long Island Sound. He wishes that she had asked him to walk with her, to sit on one of the park benches there and look out at the water together.

Instead he goes inside the shop. He doesn't see Jeremy at first, just his car, but Jake knows where he is. In the alley. Pipe in hand. Waiting to buy a bag of weed to make himself feel better.

Right now that sounds like a damn good idea to Jake. Anything to get Ms. Dupré's words and the images on those tarot cards out of his mind. Anything to stop wondering about the dangerous, sharp things lurking within.

2
LISTS

Emma doesn't want to tutor Susann Roberts today. She'd rather spend more time reading the book Jake just gave her, but that's not all. If someone asked Emma to list all the things wrong with Susann, that would be easy. She would start with the obvious: Cheerleader. Susann tells everyone at school that the only reason she joined the cheerleading squad is because of Mr. Shank, the guidance counselor who advised her to take up a few more extracurriculars for her college applications.

"You know, I took ballet as a kid. I like all kinds of dance, *really.*" Susann has said this about a hundred million times, and it always comes out in the same annoying way. Her voice rises a bit with the word "really"—as if this were the most surprising and important revelation of the twenty-first century.

Emma doesn't buy it.

First of all, cheerleading isn't dancing. Cheerleading is jumping up and down and looking like an idiot in front of a few hundred people during basketball games. Second, Susann enjoys it way too much. She likes having so many people watch her. Sure, Susann isn't quite as pretty as Kristine and Dana, and she isn't as cheerful as Brandie, who smiles so much you want to punch her in the face. *I mean, no one can be in such a good mood all the time,* Emma says to herself. *No way.* But still, Susann is one of the best-looking and most popular girls at school, and that's reason enough to dislike her.

So, back to Emma's list of all the things wrong with Susann Roberts:

1. Cheerleader
2. Fashion-Model Looks—Blond Hair, Blue Eyes, Big Breasts
3. Perfect Body

Emma passes Memorial Park and turns down Tilley Place. Her mom used to keep lists for everything, she thinks. For groceries. For Christmas gifts. For Emma's and Gwen's chores. For all the things Dad was supposed to do around the house but usually forgot—like recycling, mowing the lawn, and taking out the garbage on Wednesday night.

And there was the list of all her medication.

Her mom's cancer knocked the entire Montgomery house sideways. It no longer revolved around Emma and Gwen. Her mom stopped coming into their rooms every morning to wake them up for school. She stopped leaving brown-bag lunches on the kitchen table next to the big blue cookie jar. And she stopped taking them to school. Dad drove sometimes, or they just carpooled with the Everton family next door. Emma preferred going with the Evertons, since Dad slammed on the brakes and honked the horn a lot.

Sometimes Emma remembers her mom's pills more clearly than anything else during those five months. She can still list all of their colors (blue, red, yellow, white, orange) and see all of their shapes (oval, circular, five-sided, eight-sided, rectangular). Her mom kept lists for doctors' appointments and treatments—all of which got longer and longer. She created charts telling her when to take certain pills and when not to take others.

She used to say that lists can remind you that the world isn't such a big place after all, that small things matter.

Several weeks after she died, those lists were still on the table by her bed, alongside the untaken pills and her reading glasses with the purple frames. Neither Dad nor Gwen nor Emma could bring themselves to touch those things for a long time. It was all they really had left of her—unfinished lists.

In some way that's why Emma likes lists. They can go on forever. If she ever kept a diary, Emma would number all the lines. That's what her diary would look like. One long list after another. No paragraphs and sentences. Those things end. Lists can stay unfinished.

Case in point: her list of all the things wrong with Susann Roberts. With each step toward Susann's house, it gets longer:

1. Cheerleader
2. Fashion-Model Looks—Blond hair, Blue Eyes, Big Breasts
3. Perfect Body
4. Cheerleader
5. Not Very Smart
6. Cheerleader
7. <u>Putting the Moves on Jake Hardale</u>

This last one has been a recent development, and it worries Emma the most. Ever since she and Jake started spending time together, Susann has been all over him at school. Flirting in the halls. Texting him during Dr. Beecher's class. Having lunch with Emma and Jake on the bench near the chapel. Susann is always hitting on some guy and then dropping him a few weeks later. But Jake isn't falling for it. No. He doesn't get caught up in the games at school—the popularity contests, the gossip. Emma likes that about him. It's as if he's part of things but outside of them at the same time. This is how she has felt about everything since her mom died. Apart. Outside.

Still, Susann could date anyone in school. There isn't a guy at Saint Opportuna who doesn't check her out when she walks across the schoolyard. So why is she toying with Jake Hardale—the first guy Emma has liked since moving to Sea Cliff last spring? Jake, who wears the same outfit to school every day: a black T-shirt and black jeans. Jake, who never seems to get all the grease out from underneath his fingernails. Jake, who hooked up with Caitlin Harris in New Orleans. And Jake, who gave her a copy of *The Sun Also Rises* just a few minutes ago.

Jake.

On the surface he seems like a slacker, but there's a real depth to Jake. She first noticed it in New Orleans. Sensitive. Thoughtful. Sweet. Sure, she's not crazy about the fact that he gets high all the time. She's heard the talk around school—about him being a major dealer in town as well as a total stoner. She doesn't mind that he smokes. Not really. She knows there is more to him than that, even if other people can't see it.

Emma opens the book again and rereads the epigraph by Gertrude Stein: "You are all a lost generation."

She wishes Jake had written an inscription. It's not that she wants some cheesy poem about the color of her eyes or a clumsy outpouring of feelings; that wouldn't be like Jake anyway. She just wants to see his handwriting—to know what it looks like when he's writing to her. It wouldn't be sloppy and illegible, she decides. Not rounded and flowery like Susann's, either. No, his writing would be small and tight. The letters close together on the page. Direct. Meaningful.

Yes, Emma would have liked that.

She hasn't been paying much attention to her walk toward Susann's until she stumbles on the loose gravel, almost dropping the book. The steep incline of Tilley Place is always tricky. It makes the street seem as if it might spill right into the Sound, but it stops abruptly at the cliff's edge—where Susann's house is and where a wooden staircase descends to the pier. Emma shuffles down the rest of the hill and pauses in front of the last house: a bluish-gray Victorian with maroon trim. A few tiles are missing from the pointed roof, and a brick chimney leans away from the house as if it's ready to pull itself free.

Emma wonders what it would be like to live in a house that hangs partway over the edge of a cliff. Would you always be aware that you're not on solid ground—walking through rooms on tiptoe and being careful not to drop anything? Would you worry about the floors giving way and slipping out from underneath your feet?

Emma carefully tucks the book in her backpack and climbs up the narrow steps of the Roberts house. She knocks on the door.

"Come in," Susann says as she pulls the door open and turns around. A pink skirt flutters around her waist.

Emma immediately thinks of one more entry for her list of all the things wrong with Susann Roberts: *Pink Clothes.*

Every week Emma helps Susann with her homework for English class, and Mrs. Roberts pays her fifteen dollars an hour.

Of course Susann would prefer if Emma just did the work for her. She'd also prefer if Emma wrote the papers, did the reading, took the quizzes, and attended class for her, but that's another story.

As soon as they sit next to each other at the dining room table, Susann stares at the mostly empty notebook in front of her.

"I can't do this today," she says, her head still down. The golden curls of her hair almost touch the table.

"It's just a poetry explication," Emma begins. "We can get through it in no time. Robert Frost isn't so—"

"You don't understand. I . . ." Susann hesitates.

"What?"

Susann looks up, and Emma notices her eyes for the first time today. They're bloodshot and heavy.

"I haven't been sleeping," Susann says. "For days, really. I just . . . I just can't sleep anymore."

The sincerity in Susann's voice startles Emma. She is used to the pink, popular, perfect-looking Susann. She is used to the Susann who has probably never known one day of real sadness and pain in her life. But this Susann makes Emma uneasy.

"Maybe you could take some sleeping pills or something—"

"I can't do that either."

"Why not?"

"I *can't* sleep!" Susann slaps the table with her right hand, and the sound echoes loudly in the tall room. "If I do, weird things happen. I mean . . . my body does things."

Emma hesitates. "What kind of things?"

Susann shakes her head. "Twice this week my mom has found me standing in the kitchen," she says without looking at Emma. Her eyes have returned to the blank pages in front of her. "Both times at like three in the morning."

"So?"

"Each time, I've filled the sink with water. I'm standing in front of it. Looking down. Then I stick my face into the water and start screaming."

"What?"

"Most of the sound is muffled, I guess. My mom . . . she hears the running water. She woke me up both times, but I don't remember any of it."

A few teardrops flatten on the white paper, and Emma can hear Susann sniffle. The coolness of the room gives Emma a sudden chill. Selene Johnson used to sleepwalk too, she thinks. Until the night they found Reverend Michaels's body, the night they all promised to keep it a secret. *"We came here to build a home for Calliope Johnson and her daughter, Selene. To help them start a new life,"* Dr. Beecher said by the stone angel in the graveyard. *"We can't take that away from them. Not after everything that's happened."*

Susann sniffles again, and Emma reaches for her hand. They are quiet for a while after that—just holding hands and sitting still. Emma gets a sick, sinking feeling in her stomach from thinking about New Orleans, from knowing about the terrible thing that happened that night. She glances at Susann and wonders if she needs to make a new list called "What's Surprising About Susann Roberts." She knows how it would start:

1. Cheerleaders Aren't Always What They Seem To Be.

Example: Susann Roberts

"Maybe we should look at the first poem," Emma suggests gently.

Susann nods as she lets go of Emma's hand. She then wipes the tears from the pages in front of her.

"I think it's called 'Desert Places,'" Emma says, taking the poetry book from her backpack and opening to the section on Robert Frost. "Let's look at the—"

"'I have it in me so much nearer home,'" Susann recites, "'To scare myself with my own desert places.'" She pauses and looks directly at Emma. Her blue eyes glimmer with water. "I understand that one."

With that, Emma realizes that she definitely has to work on a new list for Susann Roberts.

THURSDAY

3
THE LAZARUS CLUB

At first it only drips, drips, drips.

Slowly. Steadily. A few drops splatter against his lips and on his nose. But most of them fill his mouth. He can taste the thick, bitter motor oil coating his tongue and pushing its way into his throat. He spits out as much as he can, but the drops come faster now. They are falling from somewhere high above him.

Drip drip drip drip . . .

He struggles to turn his head, to lift himself up, to pull free. But his entire body is trapped. He has been fastened to a hard table, but he can't see how it was done. Only his eyes can move. He looks from side to side, trying to see anything other than the blackness of the room. There is a faint sound in the far corner. Someone moaning in pain, he thinks.

Drip drip dr—

The drops turn into a stream now. Filling his mouth. Covering his face. He can't breathe. He can't call out for help.

The moaning gets louder.

He swallows a mouthful, and it burns his throat. There is no more air, he realizes. Only oil. Oil everywhere . . .

Drowning him.

Jake wakes up, coughing violently. He rolls out of bed and hurries into the bathroom. He spits into the sink a few times, then laps up water from the faucet. He has been having variations of this nightmare for several days. Sometimes his body is being lowered slowly into a vat of oil—facedown—and he watches the smooth, black surface until it swallows him. Other times drops of motor oil cover his face until he feels it thickening in his mouth.

Jake steps back into the bedroom. The clock on his dresser reads 6:47. *Good,* he thinks. At least he won't have to try going back to sleep. He can get ready for school and be the first one downstairs this morning. Of course, Jake's parents might spontaneously combust if they find him at the kitchen table drinking orange juice and reading the newspaper. For starters, he's never done that in his life. Second, he's never gotten up before them either. But maybe messing with them will get his mind off these nightmares, Jake thinks.

Usually the only time Jake surprises his parents is by finding new ways to disappoint them. His black outfits, which his mom calls "the most unfortunate and unoriginal form of teenage rebellion in town." The D- in Mr. Plotsky's chemistry class last semester. ("If you're going to fail, Jake, at least have the common sense to get an F. That way no one will think you tried in the first place," his father said before taking a long sip of wine at the dinner table.) The time he smashed a hole in his bedroom wall with a hammer. And of course the day his mother found four marijuana plants growing near her azalea bush.

"What are these?"

"I don't know," Jake replied with a shrug after she dragged him into the backyard. "I'm not good with nature."

"Don't lie to me," she said, half crying and yelling at the same time. "Are you a drug addict?"

"No."

"Go to your room!"

In some ways, Jake has gotten used to disappointing his parents. It's not that they don't love him. He can tell that they do, but they can't quite let themselves love him for who he is. Somehow, they think his "bad" choices make them bad parents.

Jake gets dressed quickly. The sight of his unmade bed makes him worry if he'll ever sleep again. Then he wonders if it's too early in the day to take a few hits from his bong—to help him mellow out. His father once said that an alcoholic is someone who drinks before noon. Maybe the same thing applies to smoking weed, Jake considers. But before he can decide what to do, he hears his mother shuffling around in the kitchen, running water for the coffee pot and opening the fridge.

"Damn," he mutters. "So much for spontaneous combustion."

Jake figures that he still has the meeting at Dr. Beecher's house tonight to look forward to. Even though they have only been getting together for a few weeks, he has gotten used to going, to working on their senior project there, and to being in Dr. Beecher's dark, strange house, near Emma. He likes that part the best.

Jake leaves the bong on his desk, tucks his iPod and cell phone inside his backpack, and walks downstairs.

While he's working on a car after school, Jake thinks about Dr. Beecher's place. It reminds him of a castle—or at least something out of a fairy tale. A mustard-colored exterior with forest-green gutters. Pointed roofs. Two brick chimneys. Windows of different shapes and sizes, all with crimson trim. A wraparound porch. And a turret that would be perfect for imprisoning a princess with long blond hair. Jake has lost count of the number of times he has walked past this house. Every time, he stops and marvels at some newly discovered detail.

"This house, like so many Victorians in the late 1800s, was built according to the Queen Anne style, which was in vogue at the time," Dr. Beecher explained to them at the first meeting. He went on to say that in the 1970s this architectural style was nicknamed Painted Lady because of its colors.

Painted Ladies can be found on practically every street in Sea Cliff. Some of them look grand and elegant like Dr. Beecher's. Others are small and quiet, worn down from years of hot summer sun and neglect. For Jake these houses are like everything else here: different degrees of old. Beautiful at times, sure. But old. As far as Jake can tell, the town of Sea Cliff would have preferred if the nineteenth century had never ended.

Jake glances at his watch.

"Damn," he mutters, looking at the grease on his hands and the 1965 Dodge Dart raised on the lift. He has been at Island Auto longer than he expected. Mr. Tatonetti refuses to leave until the brake pads on his car are replaced.

"I've been waiting two days," he barked. "No more!"

Mr. Tatonetti can't tell an exhaust pipe from a spark plug, but he's one of those men who stares at an engine long enough to make most other folks think he knows something about cars.

Loser.

Jake hurries to replace the brake pads, but by the time he finishes up, he's already fifteen minutes late for the meeting.

"Damn."

Dr. Beecher despises tardiness. In class he gives out detention slips for the slightest infraction of his on-time rule, whether you're ten minutes or one second late. Of course, Dr. Beecher won't hand out detention tonight, but Jake starts to worry about what might happen instead. Will he be kicked out of the group? The thought makes his stomach drop. Sometimes Jake wonders if he'd be better off without them—avoiding all contact and just trying to forget what happened in New Orleans. But he's not sure he could cope with the bad memories and feelings alone. They all went through the same thing there.

They all saw Reverend Michaels's body.

Jake runs down Prospect Street, hurrying toward the mustard-colored Victorian which seems to stretch higher into the sky with each step. Jake turns in to the walk and bounds up the steps to the front door. It's unlocked.

Inside, the foyer leads to a short hallway. To his right there is a wooden staircase that corkscrews up to the second floor. The carvings on the handrail resemble vines, and in several places the varnish shines from years of touch. An entryway on the left opens into the living room. The entire house is dimly lit. Only the yellow glow of candles brightens the room.

Jake's eyes take a moment to adjust.

Above the brick fireplace at the far end of the living room is a blank screen where the paintings and photographs will be projected. Thick drapes cover the windows, and the rest of the walls seem crowded with bookcases. A circular wooden table occupies the center of the room. Several chairs and a couch have been placed around it. Dr. Beecher and Caitlin are sitting close together on the couch.

Caitlin stopped talking to Jake after their trip to New Orleans, as if it was okay to be with him in a strange place for a while but not where they really live, not where other people at school could see them together. He tries not to be hurt by this—by going from strangers to lovers to strangers all over again. But rejection always sucks, especially the silent, cold-shoulder kind. Sure, he knew it wouldn't last. She is too beautiful for him, Jake admits. His look—the black clothes, greasy hair, and slightly crooked nose—doesn't fly with most of the students at Saint Opportuna, who dress like they live at Banana Republic. But still, he didn't expect to be erased from her life so fast.

Jake doesn't want her anymore. Not really. But he doesn't like seeing her next to Dr. Beecher on the couch. He's heard the rumors going around school, but he doesn't want to believe them. Not her and Dr. Beecher. No way.

The leather chair on Dr. Beecher's right seems to be swallowing Emma. She leans forward and smiles at Jake as soon as he enters. The tingling feeling in his stomach returns. He gets it every time he sees Emma, and he likes it. He never felt that way with Caitlin. Duncan Boyce slouches in the chair next to Emma, and Lily Ambrose sits next to him.

"Now that Mr. Hardale is here, perhaps we can look at a painting," Dr. Beecher says, glancing at an empty chair. Every week he begins with one painting, "as a way to warm up," he tells them. "To get you thinking about images." Although Jake seems to remember that it was Caitlin who first suggested this idea, that doesn't change the fact that it reminds him way too much of school. Still, he has to admit that it feels different looking at this stuff in Dr. Beecher's house. It seems more adult. And Jake likes that.

Even in his own home Dr. Beecher dresses formally: in one of his signature three-piece suits (today it's white), with polished dress shoes, a colorful silk handkerchief tucked in his breast pocket, and a matching tie. He has a neatly manicured jet-black mustache and small circular glasses that rest on his stubby nose. Jake isn't sure what people wore in the nineteenth century, but he figures that Dr. Beecher inherited his fashion sense with the house.

Jake quickly takes a seat across from Emma. The candlelight gives her skin a golden color. Her features are soft and shimmering. He wishes he had gotten here earlier. Last week they both sat on the couch, where he could brush up against her and feel her weight against his body when she laughed.

"Caitlin," Dr. Beecher says, and she immediately hops off the couch and steps over to the slide projector.

Dr. Beecher doesn't believe in computers or PowerPoint presentations or anything else technological, so he lets Caitlin prepare all the slides on some equipment in a computer lab at school. Like his house and his clothes, Dr. Beecher only uses ancient things. The clunky projector has a carousel on top for individual slides—just like the one he has in class. As soon as Caitlin turns on the machine, it hums loudly.

"Remember," Dr. Beecher says cheerfully, "I want you to clear your mind of everything else. Homework. Checking your phone for text messages."

Everyone smiles.

"Okay," Dr. Beecher says to Caitlin, and the light from the projector throws the first image onto the screen with a loud click.

A skeletal, twisted body is trying to pull itself out of a tomb. Several onlookers cower in the corner. And a tall man stands above them all. He wears thick blue garments. His mouth is open as if calling out, and his right hand is raised above his head. To Jake it looks like he is pulling the skeletal body up with imaginary strings—as if it were a puppet.

"Someone is getting out of a coffin," Caitlin calls out. Her raspy voice cracks slightly, and Jake glances at her. In the white light of the projector he can see her shoulder-length blond hair and the shape of her thin, muscular frame.

"He's wearing white," Caitlin continues.

"A shroud," Duncan blurts out.

Duncan sits very still in his chair, and his shirt, which is always buttoned to the top, makes him look perpetually uncomfortable. His dark hair is parted neatly and very dorkily to the right, Jake notes.

"Yes, yes," Dr. Beecher adds eagerly. "Impressive. Now, think of all the things—television commercials, websites, magazine ads, billboards—that you see every day. Think of all the things that you look at without giving a second thought. But all of those images, all of those pictures have layers of messages and meanings. Just like this one."

Dr. Beecher leans back on the couch and rests his arms across his stomach. "What else do you see?"

"The man standing over everything," Lily adds sheepishly. Her long red-brown hair and thick glasses hide most of her face.

"Is that supposed to be Jesus?" Emma asks without looking away from the painting.

"Yes. This is Rembrandt's depiction of Jesus raising Lazarus from the dead," Dr. Beecher says. "Turning death into life."

"I don't understand," Emma continues. "If all of those people watching are like Lazarus's family and friends, why aren't they happier?"

"Very good, Emma." Dr. Beecher nods vigorously. "Very good!"

Sometimes Dr. Beecher's enthusiasm makes Jake think of a game-show host, but there is something about his round body, silly clothes, and wide smile that is contagious.

"Change is never easy," Dr. Beecher continues. "It's often a painful, violent thing. Notice the sword hanging on the wall—a reminder of the violent acts that begin and end our lives. Birth. Death."

"And Jesus will be crucified, too," Duncan adds.

Jake shifts uncomfortably in his seat. He hasn't said anything yet, and he wonders if anyone else has noticed. They all talk so easily about art. When Jake looks at paintings, he sees the shapes and colors. He admires the stories they tell. But going beyond that doesn't come naturally to him. Besides, he wonders how they can look at Lazarus and not think of Reverend Michaels in that grave. Are they just caught up in the painting? Or have all these months of rationalizing and trying to forget started to erase the past?

Suddenly, Jake's throat gets dry.

"Yes," Dr. Beecher says to Duncan. "Change is not only

painful, but it leads to more significant things. In this case the Crucifixion." Dr. Beecher pauses, closing his eyes for a moment and exhaling audibly. "Okay . . . let's have a toast."

He gets up from the couch and steps over to a small table by the foyer. A silver tray with a bottle of red wine and six silver chalices rests on top. Dr. Beecher lifts it carefully and brings it to the coffee table in the middle of their circle. He fills the glasses in silence and passes them around.

If the parents at Saint Opportuna knew about this part of the meetings, they'd freak out, Jake thinks with a smirk. Actually, they'd refuse to believe it at first. Everyone in town loves Dr. Beecher, who is a former college professor and director of the Community Service Center at school. He runs food drives for the homeless. He takes students on trips with Habitat for Humanity, and he even gets some of the slackers to volunteer at the Literacy Outreach Program in Huntington. He's a town celebrity.

Once everyone has a chalice, he begins the incantation:

Sons of Hypnos,
The gods who bring dreams into the world,
Bring us rest.

They all raise their cups and say:

Bring us rest.

Jake takes a big swig, and the wine tastes thick and peppery on his tongue. He finds this chanting stuff pretty lame, but after it, they'll talk and joke around a bit. Then they'll look through photos for their New Orleans project and try to remember good things about the trip. He glances at Emma with a smile. Dr. Beecher continues:

Ease our conscience.

Once again, everyone echoes:

Ease our conscience.

Jake takes another swig.

And bring us the strength to live without guilt and fear.

They all lift their chalices one last time. Dr. Beecher takes a sip of wine and clears his throat. "So . . . how are things?"

There is a long silence.

"It's easy to tell ourselves not to feel guilty," Dr. Beecher says, "but in my experience guilt doesn't listen very well. It doesn't like to be told what to do." He smiles. "I keep thinking about all the good you've done. Building homes for those people in New Orleans. Helping them survive." Dr. Beecher's eyes widen, and Jake can see Lily nodding.

"That's what you've done," Dr. Beecher continues. "You've helped save lives. That's what you need to remember."

He pauses, but before anyone can respond, the phone rings. The harsh, abrupt sound makes everyone jump.

"I'm sorry." Dr. Beecher clears his throat. "Excuse me for just a moment."

He gets up from the couch and steps over to a table in the back corner of the living room.

Jake looks at Lazarus again, and the painting makes him

think about how secrets don't usually stay buried. No matter how hard you try. Maybe that's what they should call their secret society, he tells himself: the Lazarus Club.

Dr. Beecher hangs up the phone and is silent for a few moments. He walks back to the circle.

"Do all of you know Jeremy Carson from our class?" he asks.

Everyone nods, and Jake pipes up, still feeling warm and good from the wine, "Yeah, I fixed his car yesterday."

Dr. Beecher, who is now standing next to Emma's chair, stares at him for a moment.

"He died."

4

MAGIC WAND

Emma can still remember when her parents had magic powers.

As soon as she and Gwen were ready for bed, Mom and Dad would come into their room. They would lean over both girls for a kiss, pull the covers a little higher, and turn off the light. Before leaving the room they would stand close together in the doorway, their bodies silhouettes against the light from the hallway. Then Emma's mom would take out a magic wand and wave it across the doorway.

"With this wand I take away all the bad dreams in this room," she would say every night.

And it worked. Emma can't remember having one bad dream during her childhood.

A few months after her mom died, Emma found an old cardboard box in the hall closet. She wasn't snooping around; she was just looking for an umbrella. That's when she came across a box filled with photographs, old baby shoes, silver-plated rattles, ticket stubs for airline tickets to France and Spain, and the magic wand.

The thin piece of black plastic with its white tip felt so light in her hands. It looked silly, Emma thought. How could she have believed that such a cheap toy had so much power? That it could make things better?

Despite these thoughts Emma waved it in the air really fast and said, "With this wand I want Mom back."

After that she threw it back in the box. She never touched it again.

Ever since the news tonight of Jeremy Carson's death, Emma has been thinking about that wand—wishing that there were enough magic in the world to undo painful things. Of course, she hardly knew Jeremy. She has only been living in Sea Cliff and going to Saint Opportuna for ten months. Her dad packed up the house and moved her and Gwen to Long Island four months after the funeral. He just couldn't live in North Carolina anymore.

"Everything here reminds me of your mother," he told Emma one night. "The trees. The way the ground smells after a thunderstorm. Everything. We've got to go."

That's how she came to this place in the middle of her junior year in high school. She was angry then—about Mom, about leaving her friends, about losing Ms. Gregson as her piano teacher, and about selling the house she grew up in. But after her dad said those words, Emma didn't complain anymore. She's not exactly sure why. Maybe she just hopes that someone will love her that much one day.

So when Dr. Beecher told everyone that Jeremy had died in a car accident—losing control somehow and hitting a tree—she saw the pained expression on Jake's face. She wanted to make it better somehow. She wanted to wish it away. But she didn't even get to talk to him afterward. The meeting ended early, and Jake rushed out of the house as if he were sick to his stomach.

Jeremy had always seemed nice. He played Henry Higgins in the school's production of *My Fair Lady* last spring, though Emma didn't see it. After that he told everyone that he wanted to study acting in Manhattan after high school. Off-Broadway theater, that's where he'd end up, he said. In their English class Emma thought Jeremy was a little too into reading the passages aloud (changing his voice and getting all theatrical), but Ms. Robeson ate it up. Still, he said hi to Emma in the halls and smiled lots.

The news about Jeremy makes her sad, but she can't stop worrying about Jake. For the last two weeks he has walked her home from Dr. Beecher's place, and she was looking forward to that again. To navigating the narrow streets of Sea Cliff with him. To brushing against him every few steps. To wondering if it would happen this time, if he would finally stop and kiss her.

Instead she heads down Main Street with Duncan and Lily tonight. None of them are very talkative, and they walk for a long time in silence. A heaviness hangs over them, and it's a feeling they shared in New Orleans, Emma remembers. A feeling that makes her worry that something bad is going to happen. . . .

As Reverend Michaels hurried up the street, he reminded Emma of the stick figures she and Gwen used to draw as kids. Big, round head. Boxy rectangles for feet. Arms and legs that were toothpick thin. But unlike their drawings this man wore a flowing white robe and carried an enormous Bible as if he had just finished preaching.

Emma glanced at Duncan and Lily to see if they had noticed him, but they were concentrating on the trench. Duncan's face was already shiny with sweat, and Lily, with her drooping shoulders, looked as if she might collapse at any second. The three of them were digging up part of the yard to lay pipes from the house to the septic tank. Caitlin and Jake were inside, working on the floorboards with Dr. Beecher and some of the other people from Habitat.

"Good morning!" Reverend Michaels called out cheerfully.

His voice made him sound about two hundred pounds heavier, Emma thought. The cello vibrations of each word. The sudden shift from loud to soft. Of course, you couldn't help but notice his voice, since he talked so much—about the Lord, about the fine city of N'Awlins, about the good work of rebuilding.

"I thought I'd come on by and start you off with a prayer today," he said, putting his hand on Emma's shoulder.

She, Duncan, and Lily looked at each other, and Emma was convinced that they were all thinking the same thing: If you want to help, pick up a shovel. But none of them spoke.

"Y'all go to Catholic school, right?" he asked playfully. "So I figure you've heard of prayer."

With that, Reverend Michaels took a step back and opened the Bible to read. "When the possessed man saw Jesus, he cried out, 'What have I to do with thee, Jesus, thou Son of God most high? I beseech thee, torment me not.' (For Jesus had commanded the unclean spirit to come out of the man.) And Jesus asked him, saying, 'What is thy name?' And he said, 'Legion': because many devils were entered into him."

His words suddenly got lost in a fit of coughing that shook his entire body. He kept moving his lips, but no sound came out. Then blood poured from his nostrils in steady, thick streams—over his lips and down his chin. He dropped the Bible with a yell and started to shake more violently.

"Reverend?" Lily cried out.

Reverend Michaels yelled again, this time much louder. And Emma could see that his eyes were bleeding too. Blood pooled underneath his eyelids and spilled out from both sides. His pupils turned red.

"I can't see!" he screamed.

A new pain must have seized his body, because he grabbed his lower back, and the muscles in his face tightened. He fell to the ground, arching his back like a bow. He clenched his teeth, and his lips started to turn purple.

Before Emma could move, Dr. Beecher was by his side. He tried to hold Reverend Michaels still by the shoulders, but he kept losing his grip. Jake and Caitlin ran up to the reverend's convulsing body too. They were alongside Mr. Yanosh, the director of Habitat, who immediately took charge.

"Let's get him to his feet. It's faster if we drive him to the hospital," he said to Dr. Beecher.

Dr. Beecher and Mr. Yanosh helped the reverend off the ground and began leading him to a car. A moment later the car left a thin trail of dust in the air, which faded away with the sound of the engine. Lily sniffled and shook. Jake and Duncan stood next to her, staring at their feet. On the ground in front of them the Bible lay open to the book of Luke. Drops of blood stained the page.

Caitlin was no longer with them, Emma realized. She turned toward the house and saw her there. Caitlin had picked up a rag doll that had lain on the ground beside several bags of cement. She held it in both hands as if it were something fragile.

"Caitlin?" Emma called out.

Caitlin glanced up from the doll and then brought it over to the rest of them.

The doll was filthy and oddly shaped. It looked like a long time had passed since a little girl had loved it, Emma thought. Then she noticed the pins. One in the nose. One in each eye. Two in the lower back.

They all stood in a circle around the doll in Caitlin's hands. None of them spoke at first.

"Do you think this . . . ," Caitlin began, then stopped herself. She looked up at Jake. "Is it possible?"

She pulled out the pins—cautiously, one at a time—and dropped them to the ground. . . .

Around the campfire later that night, Dr. Beecher told them that the reverend's pain had gone away before they got to the hospital. "It was like someone threw a switch and he was all better," Dr. Beecher said in disbelief. "Thank God."

Emma looked at Caitlin, but she just kept staring at the flames, her expression far away.

The Sea Cliff streets are getting darker, and Emma imagines that pretty soon she, Lily, and Duncan will look like shadows. Emma glances at Lily and decides to try to break the awkward silence.

"Did you guys know Jeremy?" she asks. "I mean . . . were you friends?"

"Not really," Lily replies without looking up. Her gray dress, which covers most of her body, has a shapeless quality. "He lives on my street."

"Lived," Duncan says, correcting her. He keeps close to Emma, and she can feel his hand bump against hers.

"He had a sandbox in his backyard," Lily continues, almost as if Duncan hasn't spoken; she's using the past tense now though. "And a swing. We used to have so much fun building castles and pushing each other in the swing. To see how high we could go—" Lily stops abruptly, glancing over at Emma and Duncan for the first time. "I mean, when we were really little."

"That was way before he became such a jerk," Duncan mutters.

"What do you mean?" Emma asks, surprised by his anger.

"Before he stopped talking to Lily and me in junior high. We just weren't cool enough." Duncan laughs dryly. "Neither was he, but he wanted people to think he was. The car he got at sixteen. Getting the lead in last year's play. The way he was glued to his iPhone—as if the president of the United States was going to text him at any second."

"Sometimes friends grow apart," Lily says defensively, her voice tight.

"It's not like I hated him, Lil." Duncan turns to her. "I don't care about me. He should have been nicer to you. That's all."

There is a sweetness between Duncan and Lily that Emma admires and feels envious of at the same time. She has never seen them hold hands or kiss or give any outward sign that they're dating. Maybe they're just friends. Or friends that hook up sometimes. Or maybe they're falling in love. Emma can't tell, but hearing Duncan and Lily talk makes her wish even more that Jake were here.

Emma checks her phone for messages. Nothing from Jake.

"Dr. Beecher wouldn't approve," Duncan says with a smirk, and Emma slips the phone back into her pocket.

"I know, I know," she replies playfully, but of course it's true.

"I worry about you," Dr. Beecher has told them many times. "It actually keeps me up at night, the way so many of you have retreated into a digital world. The more connected you are to phones and iPods and computer screens, the less connected you are to each other. The less human you become."

Emma isn't sure what to make of his comments. In some ways he's right. She sees people at school texting instead of talking—even when they're sitting next to each other. But her cell phone and the time she spends on MySpace make her feel connected to people too. Especially her friends back home. Dr. Beecher doesn't understand that MySpace is just that: a place that's completely hers. It's where she can be who she is, who she wants to be apart from her family.

The sun is still leaning against the horizon when the three of them get to Emma's house on Littleworth Lane: a white Victorian with a blue porch. From the sidewalk Emma can hear her sister practicing the first movement of Beethoven's G-minor sonata. Her father is sitting in his favorite chair by the front window, reading.

"I'll see you guys tomorrow," Emma says, before heading up the short brick walkway to her porch.

In her room Emma plops down at her desk to check her MySpace page for postings. She told her father about Jeremy as soon as she got home, and he gave her one of his big bear hugs. Smothering. Warm. "Are you okay?" he asked about a dozen times. His eyes were wide as he watched her, and Emma could tell what he was thinking: *Can she deal with another death so soon after losing her mother?*

Emma wonders how he would have reacted to Jeremy's death if he knew about Reverend Michaels. Maybe she's not okay after all, Emma thinks, but she didn't say this to her dad. "Don't worry, Daddy," she told him instead before slipping upstairs.

Sitting in front of her computer now, she stares at the picture on her desktop of her and Gwen with their mom at a beach in Wilmington, North Carolina. All smiles. Hair mussed up from the wind. It was a cloudy day, and the grayness in the sky made the ocean waves look gray too.

Dad took the picture. It was their last family trip together. Mom was diagnosed with cancer a week later.

As the web page is loading, Emma's screen flickers. It brightens fast, blanching the colors of the picture. The monitor buzzes with static, then goes black.

Only a shadowy reflection of her face remains on the screen. It reminds her of Lazarus from the painting—unreal, ghostly.

She presses the power button several times, but nothing happens. Pushing the chair away from her desk, she gets on her hands and knees to check the power strip underneath.

Everything is plugged in.

"Crap," she mutters.

Emma is about to call out to her dad when she notices an envelope on her bed. Someone has been in her room. Probably Gwen, though Emma has told her to stay out a million times.

As soon as Emma gets to her feet, she steps over and grabs the envelope. Her name is written in block letters: *EMMA.*

She opens it quickly, hoping it might be from Jake. He could have left it in the mailbox. Or maybe he slipped it under the front door after the meeting, and Gwen forgot to tell her that she brought it upstairs. Or maybe—

The note inside is short. It's written in the same block letters as on the envelope, but they seem ominous now. Smeared black ink. Sharp angles.

Emma's stomach cramps as she reads the words there:

IT'S COMING FOR YOU

FRIDAY

5
LIGHTNING AND SAND

The morning after Jeremy Carson slammed his car into an oak tree at Bryant Park Cemetery is a strange one for Jake. For starters he's stoned—well, that part isn't entirely surprising. He spent most of the night smoking out, eating Oreo cookies, and listening to a local radio station that was playing African drum music.

Anything to keep himself from dreaming.

He can't handle another nightmare. Not after what happened to Jeremy. Not after Ms. Dupré's tarot cards. And not after seeing that damn painting of Lazarus. Jake has been trying to figure out why that painting bothers him so much. Something about having no control over what happens to you—like the way Lazarus is being pulled out of the tomb.

Jake closes his eyes for a moment, then immediately forces them back open.

"Damn," he says aloud, trying to keep himself awake. "Just one more hour."

He has been sitting up in bed for most of the night, fully dressed and leaning against a pile of pillows. He has studied every inch of his room. Again. Classic car posters. Dirty clothes on the floor. Stacks of *Car and Driver* magazine on his computer desk. And a wooden bookcase that doesn't have any books on it—just wrenches, screwdrivers, spark plugs, hammers, coffee cans filled with nuts and bolts, and, of course, old parts from his still-not-running 1972 Plymouth Charger.

Jake's mother has been asking him to move that "car junk" into the garage for almost a year now, but he refuses. He likes having these things around. They remind him of what he does well. Fixing broken things. His dad can't repair anything around the house. Leaky faucets, loose floorboards, even burned out lightbulbs seem insurmountable for him. But fixing things comes easy for Jake.

That's why the nightmares bother him so much. It's as if something is broken inside, but he doesn't know how to fix it. Once again Jake watches the clock: 6:57 . . . 6:58 . . . 6:59 . . . 7:00. The alarm buzzes aggressively, and he turns it off with a snap.

"Made it," he says aloud. No sleep. No dreams.

He considers changing his clothes, but that seems like too much effort for his tired body. Instead Jake gets out of bed and lumbers downstairs, clothes wrinkled and legs sluggish. He walks past the gurgling coffee pot and the newspaper wrapped in plastic on the kitchen counter. He doesn't see his mother there or in the living room. But he doesn't call out to her either.

He just opens the front door and steps into the misty morning air.

Jake's first three classes are hell—even more so than usual. Kristin York and Bryan Edleman, who have been sleeping together since junior prom, are all over each other in calculus, whispering, touching, texting.

Damn annoying, Jake thinks.

Then Ms. Wright, his English teacher, gives a pop quiz, and after that Father Mike, whose spherical body and white beard make him look like Santa Claus, spends theology class asking everyone to talk through their feelings about Jeremy's death.

"It's natural to look for an explanation," Father Mike says softly. "To look for someone or something to blame. . . ."

But Jake doesn't want to talk. He feels pretty torn up about Jeremy. When they hung out together in tenth grade, Jeremy never gave Jake shit about his clothes. And he never acted differently around Jake even when he started hanging out with the more popular people at school. Jake liked him, so how is he supposed to feel about Jeremy's accident? Jake fixed his car. Sure, it was the radiator, nothing that would cause an accident like that, but still. And what if Jeremy was high when he hit that tree? Jake wonders. Everyone will know where he got the pot. Everyone will blame Jake. But the accident happened seven hours after they smoked. Seven hours!

He keeps his eyes lowered for the rest of class anyway, watching the hands on his watch crawl forward. One impossibly long second at a time.

About one hundred years later the bell rings for lunch. Jake can't get out of there fast enough.

In the courtyard he starts to feel dizzy. He wants to see Emma. Bad. Hell, he wanted to call her last night, to send her some kind of message, but he didn't know what to say. How can you tell someone about being too afraid to sleep?

Maybe this was inevitable, he thinks. Being frightened by

dreams. In New Orleans he learned that dreams are something to be afraid of. . . .

Jake dipped his sudsy rag into the bucket one more time before starting. The name PHOBETOR had been smeared in brownish red on the south wall of the house they were building, the house that would be Calliope Johnson's new home. The name MORPHEUS appeared on the west wall, and across from that someone had written PHANTASOS. When everyone from Habitat had arrived in the morning and seen the graffiti, Dr. Beecher had told Jake, Emma, and Duncan to clean it up right away. That was so not the job Jake wanted, but he could tell by the serious expression on Dr. Beecher's face that it wasn't open for discussion.

"Do you think it's from a pig?" Duncan asked.

"What?" Jake snapped.

"The blood. Do you think it's from a pig? Or maybe a chicken?"

"How the hell should I know?" Jake responded.

Duncan shrugged and started scrubbing PHANTASOS. The dried blood seemed to come off easily.

A loud crash of thunder shook the house, and Jake began wiping away the bloody letters on the wall in front of him. Another storm was rolling through New Orleans. A few bolts of lightning flared up in the dark sky, and then the heavy downpour began. The whole thing would last about fifteen or twenty minutes, Jake told himself. He knew the routine by that point. Just like he knew that the rain wouldn't make things one bit cooler. Still, he was glad for the thunder, because it kept all of them from talking—for a while at least.

Jake needed time to think. He couldn't stop replaying Dr. Beecher's explanation of the names:

"In Greek mythology Morpheus, Phobetor, and Phantasos are responsible for bringing dreams into the world," Dr. Beecher had said as he stood in the living room of the new house and studied the walls. His white linen suit was already wrinkled, and he dabbed his forehead with a dark blue handkerchief. "They are the sons of Hypnos, the god of dreams. They live in a cave near Hades. At night they emerge in the form of bats—black-winged demons, actually."

"Phobetor?" Jake echoed. "Like phobia?"

"Yes," Dr. Beecher replied. "It literally means 'frightening.'"

Everything about this trip to New Orleans was becoming frightening, Jake thought. Strange stuff had started happening after Reverend Michaels's seizure or whatever it was. Even Caitlin wasn't the same after finding that doll. She began hanging around Dr. Beecher more, asking about the history of New Orleans and voodoo. She also stopped sleeping with Jake. She moved back to the church basement with Lily, Duncan, and Emma. So Jake joined them as well.

Caitlin never explained why her feelings had changed so fast. Sure, sometimes she still flirted with him, holding his hand or caressing the back of his neck when no one else was around. But after the day Reverend Michaels went to the hospital, something inside her just dried up as far as Jake was concerned, and he was left with an emptiness in his chest. All of the stuff he didn't like about himself—not being good-looking enough or smart enough or interesting enough for her—came rushing back to him.

The word "Phobetor" was mostly gone now, but Jake could still see traces of the letters he had washed away. He scrubbed the wall harder with his rag. And faster. He wanted to wipe all the blood clean. As he was sliding the rag up and down with both hands, he felt someone touch his arm.

"Jake," Emma said softly, "it's okay. Really. We're all freaking out right now."

He stopped cleaning and looked at her—at the greenish eyes, the small birthmark on her cheek, and the shoulder-length brown hair. He dropped the rag into the bucket. "Sorry, pent-up aggression. I never liked Greek mythology."

She gave him one of her sideways smiles. "Well, I still have half a Morpheus to clean if you want to make yourself useful."

Jake laughed.

Before he could say anything else, Calliope Johnson ran into the house. Her loose cotton dress was completely drenched from the rain. Her brown skin glistened with moisture.

"Stop!" she yelled, scanning each wall. "That's for protection."

"Protection?" Duncan asked. His buttoned-up shirt was damp from the soapy, blood-stained water.

"You've seen what's going on around here," Calliope snapped as she stepped over to Duncan and took the rag from him. That's when Jake noticed her hands. They were covered with dried blood. "Someone has it out for Reverend Michaels," she continued, "and I ain't letting anything happen to me and my girl."

"Reverend Michaels?" Emma asked. "Why would anyone want to hurt him? He's helping rebuild this place."

"Not everything can be fixed," Calliope said sharply, shaking her head. "Now leave that be, you hear?"

Without waiting for an answer, she walked toward the door.

"Miss Johnson?" Duncan called out nervously, and she faced him. "This is, uh . . . Well, it's animal blood, right?"

Calliope Johnson glanced at her hands before turning around and stepping into the rain.

In the courtyard of Saint Opportuna High School, Jake heads over to the place where he and Emma have been eating lunch with Susann for the last few weeks: the bench outside the chapel, the bench underneath the stained-glass window of Jesus resisting the temptations of Satan in the desert. But neither of the girls is there.

He rushes over to Xavier Hall.

Inside, the long empty hallways and classrooms relax Jake a bit, but still he's on a mission. At the end of the first floor he takes the stairs down to the basement, which is filled with science labs and student lockers. Jake's locker contains an emergency joint for stressful occasions just like this one, and he is more than ready to light up.

As he's walking past the geology lab, he sees Duncan and Lily. She is wearing a body-length brown dress and sitting on one of the black granite tables. Her legs rock back and forth as she eats her sandwich. Duncan is staring at a case filled with rocks and minerals.

Duncan has been into geology since he was a little kid. He told Jake all about it once. He has always liked digging things up. His mom used to complain that no garden in Long Island was safe. She was right. Duncan would dig up plants and flowers and small bushes throughout the neighborhood, just to find out what was underneath. Every once in a while he tried replanting things, like putting Mrs. Thompson's rosebushes back in the ground and repacking them with soil. But none of those plants lived very long.

"It's hard to explain to someone who doesn't know anything

about geology," he explained to Jake. "There's nothing like taking a long hike and uncovering layers of *history* right under your feet. Every rock, every mineral is different. Each one has its own shape and striations—marks that can tell you about its life. Like wrinkles and scars on people, I guess."

Duncan gets excited when he talks about geology. That's why lots of kids at school make fun of him—because he'd rather look at rocks than drink beer. But you never know about passion, Jake figures. One day it hits you hard enough to break a bone. Sure, broken bones heal, but you can always tell something isn't the way it used to be.

"Hey," Jake calls out. Duncan and Lily both look up as he enters the lab. "What are you doing?"

"We always eat lunch here," Duncan says, returning his attention to the case filled with rocks and minerals. "What's your story?"

Guilt, nightmares, and jonesing for some weed, he wants to say, but he decides to keep it simple. "Have you seen Emma?"

"Nope," Lily replies while still chewing on her sandwich. "She's probably looking for you, too."

"Me? Why do you say that?"

Lily smiles and then shrugs.

"Check this out," Duncan says, stepping closer to Jake. "Sand that has turned into glass."

Duncan hands him a piece of glass no bigger than a domino. One side is smooth, and the other is bumpy and uneven. Jake can see small bubbles clustered at one end. He wants to ask Lily more about Emma—if she knows something about how

Emma feels about him. But he'll have to wait. Duncan takes rocks very seriously.

"You need a temperature of about sixteen hundred degrees Celsius to make a ten-ounce glass bottle," Duncan continues. "What you're holding was probably hit by lightning."

"Lightning?" Jake echoes.

"Yeah." Duncan smiles. "It's amazing how some things change in an instant."

As Duncan reaches for the glass, Jake tightens his grip, not wanting to let go. All of a sudden he pictures the names PHOBETOR, MORPHEUS, and PHANTASOS on the walls of the lab, written in blood. He closes his eyes.

Jake knows what it's like to be hit by lightning, he thinks. They all do.

6
THE BLINDING OF SAMSON

Emma still doesn't know who sent that note yesterday. Gwen says she left it on Emma's pillow after finding it in the mailbox. She didn't see the postman or anyone else. It was just there with the rest of the mail.

Emma opens the note again, laying it on her Spanish book. Mr. García has been going over the past-perfect tense all period, but she hasn't been listening. No matter what he writes on the chalkboard, Emma can't stop seeing those words: *IT'S COMING FOR YOU.*

Is it a threat? A bad joke? Either way Emma can't make sense of it.

She glances at her watch—only a few more minutes until lunch. She's eager to see Jake, to show him the note. He'll know what to do, Emma thinks. He'll tell her not to worry, and something about his easygoing manner will convince her. She'll feel better.

As Emma looks to see what Mr. García is writing, Susann Roberts stands up. She isn't wearing any bright colors today, Emma notices. Just a tight black top and blue jeans. Her curly blond hair falls flat against her face as she walks back toward Emma. She is carrying her Spanish textbook in both hands.

"*Dónde vas,* Miss Roberts?" Mr. García calls out, but Susann doesn't respond. With her back to him she continues for a few more steps until she reaches Emma. Her fingers clutch the book.

"What are you doing?" Emma whispers.

Susann turns toward Hickey Stevens, who sits across from Emma; he has a puzzled smirk on his face.

"You," Susann mutters to him.

Everyone at school knows about John "Hickey" Stevens, the star center on the basketball team, who has left walnut-sized marks on the necks of most of the cheerleading squad. Susann has never cared much for him, though. According to her, she is one of the few cheerleaders whose necks—and bodies—have remained unmolested by him.

"Thank God for that," she told Emma one afternoon. "He has big buckteeth anyway!"

"Miss Roberts," Mr. García says more urgently, hunching his shoulders in a way that makes his brown suit look about two sizes too small. "Class is not over—"

Suddenly, Susann swings the book at Hickey's face. It smashes flat against his nose with a snap. His head recoils. Blood sprays across the aisle, splattering on Emma's arms and the note on her desk.

Everyone in the room seems to gasp at once. Someone yells, "Holy shit!" and several students get to their feet. Mr. García races toward Susann to grab the book. Hickey covers his face with both hands, moaning. Blood pushes through the spaces between his fingers and spills down the front of his white shirt.

Mr. García touches Hickey's shoulder tentatively, telling

him to tilt his head back. "Let's get you to the nurse," he says, then looks at Susann.

She is still standing in the same spot. Perfectly still. Her face is blank, and her eyes are glazed over and heavy.

"What—," Mr. García begins, but something about Susann's expression stops him.

"Emma," he says instead, "why don't you escort Susann to the principal's office. I'll meet you there."

The noon bell rings, and the harsh sound quiets the room. Everyone is standing now, staring at Susann and Hickey and all the blood still pouring from his nose.

"Class is dismissed," Mr. García announces. "Come on. *Vamanos*!"

The room empties quickly.

Mr. García then leads Hickey to the school nurse, and Emma is left behind with Susann.

"I need to wash this off first," Emma says, still looking at her arms.

A long string of blood and several drops have fallen on the note as well. She tries to wipe them off with her hand before tucking the note in her pocket, but the blood smears across the paper.

"What happened?" Emma mutters as she heads toward the door, holding her sticky hands away from her body. "Did you and Hickey—?" She turns to see Susann standing in the same spot. "Hey?"

Susann blinks.

"Susann?"

"Yeah," she replies hoarsely.

"Are you . . ." Emma stops for a moment, suddenly uneasy about Susann's odd silence and vacant stare. "Are you okay?"

"Me?" Susann asks with a hint of surprise. "You're the one bleeding."

"This isn't my blood," Emma says tentatively, wondering if Susann is kidding. "It's Hickey's, remember?"

Susann squints in confusion, and then her eyes fill with tears. "Remember what?"

Inside the darkened tent a fat man struggles against the soldiers holding him down. His entire body writhes in pain—back arched, fists and toes clenched, legs kicking. His face is lined like dry, cracked mud. One of the soldiers drives a knife into the fat man's right eye, but he can still see with the other. He can see the woman, his lover, running out of the tent with scissors in one hand and some of his hair in the other.

She has betrayed him.

This is the first painting that Dr. Beecher shows after lunch: Rembrandt's *The Blinding of Samson.*

Emma closes her eyes for a moment. She feels nauseated after this morning, after spending most of the last hour in Principal Mackey's office. He wanted Emma to stay until Mr. García arrived—to make sure she hadn't been involved in the fight somehow. So she and Susann sat in chairs on the opposite side of his enormous oak desk and waited. The smell in the room reminded Emma of the air fresheners her dad gets from the car wash.

Susann didn't say a word when Mr. García came in and explained that Hickey's nose was broken.

"An ambulance is here to take him to the hospital," he said, somewhat out of breath. "It looks bad."

Principal Mackey asked Susann to explain what had happened between her and John Stevens. His voice was calm and steady at first, but his face quickly reddened at her unwillingness to speak.

"Nothing," she said finally.

"You broke his nose. I wouldn't call that nothing."

"I didn't do anything," she insisted. A few tears slid down her face, and she lowered her head.

"I've called your parents," Principal Mackey continued in a hard, percussive tone. "They're coming to take you home. We'll discuss the length of your suspension when they arrive."

He looked at Emma as if he had forgotten that she was there. He dismissed her right after that. Susann didn't look up when Emma whispered good-bye. She remained perfectly still—her hands resting heavily in her lap and her shoulders curled forward as if she were slowly deflating.

Emma closed the door behind her.

"Miss Montgomery?" Dr. Beecher calls out, and Emma opens her eyes, startled to find herself in class. A green tie offsets his black pin-striped suit and matching vest. He uses his thumb and index finger to flatten his black mustache.

"So what do you see in this painting?" he asks with an encouraging smile.

She glances at Jake, who has been silent and sullen ever since he stepped into class. She then looks at Samson's tortured body again.

"He didn't see it coming," Emma says.

"What?"

"All the violence against him," Emma continues. "I don't know. It doesn't seem like he expected it."

Dr. Beecher flattens his moustache again. "I guess we're all somewhat blind to the bad things that can happen to us."

"Or the bad things we're capable of," Jake adds. His voice is dry.

"True . . . ," Dr. Beecher says as he steps away from the podium. "But maybe we should talk more about Samson. Wasn't he supposed to be the strongest man in the kingdom? It looks to me like he has really let himself go. What's that all about? Does he just need Weight Watchers or something?"

A few people laugh.

Dr. Beecher continues like that for a while until the last few minutes of class. He always reserves the end of class for a slide show. Caitlin Harris gets up from her prized seat in the front of the room, turns off the lights, and changes the carousel on the ancient slide machine.

As Emma watches her, she thinks that Caitlin has always been a little too popular with the guys. Her straight blond hair and blue eyes. Her athletic body. But it's her behavior around Dr. Beecher that has most of the students talking. They all think she's having sex with him.

"Some messed-up crush," Susann once said. But Emma thinks it's more than that. Something about the way he makes her feel important.

"Ready, Dr. Beecher," she says from the slide machine.

The lights in the room go dark. The hum and click of the

slide show begin. Every few seconds one of the paintings that they have discussed in class flashes on the screen, but no one is allowed to speak.

"It's a time to look. To concentrate. To think about what you see differently this time," Dr. Beecher has told them.

So the class watches in silence while the ancient projector hums.

Click.

The screen goes white and then *The Blinding of Samson* appears.

Click.

A new flash of whiteness is replaced by *The Raising of Lazarus.*

Click . . . click . . . click . . .

Soon Emma's eyes get heavier and heavier—until the bell rings harshly, and class is over.

SATURDAY

7
SLEEPWALKING

His bare feet sink unevenly into the sand with each step. Small stones and broken shells dig into his skin. A row of five fishing poles lines the shore, handles buried in the sand. They tilt toward the water, pulled by shiny, thin wires that disappear into the rough waves.

He walks toward the abandoned boathouse. It sits on rotting stilts, six or seven feet above the ground. The word STOP *appears on the boarded-up door. The letters bleed from the red spray paint.*

On the other side of the house he sees a girl lying on her stomach in the sand. Short black hair. Sunglasses. Faint music can be heard from her headphones.

She isn't aware of him—not until he strikes the back of her head with a broken plank.

He presses her face into the sand. Blood from her mouth slides up her cheek. She struggles to get away. Crawling. Grabbing handfuls of sand to pull herself forward. Screaming until he pushes her head into the ocean water.

Until she stops moving.

The ocean seems to moan as it carries away her body. He turns and passes underneath the boathouse again. The word STOP *is no longer on the door. And one of the fishing poles—with its nearly invisible wire and baited hook—is gone too.*

Only four remain.

Jake wakes up with a start. Out of breath. Heart pounding loud and fast. He is in his own bed, underneath the covers, but he doesn't remember getting here.

He stayed at Island Auto late to finish repairing the carburetor for Mr. Lightmore's 1966 Chrysler. There was some pizza in the office fridge, and he lay down on Hiram's couch to rest his eyes for a bit. But he doesn't remember anything after that. Not walking home. Not taking off his clothes and climbing into bed. And he sure doesn't remember letting himself fall asleep.

This nightmare is new. It's even worse than the others, which Jake didn't think was possible.

"So what's next?" he mutters aloud. Dreams about nuclear war? An outbreak of the Ebola virus? Sitting through another Reese Witherspoon movie?

But none of his joking helps. He can't laugh this off. His heart is still racing, and sweat is beading on his forehead. How could he dream of doing that to someone? And who is that girl? She looks so familiar. Someone from school, maybe. He's not sure.

Jake's throat gets dry, and he swallows hard. Next to him the bedside clock reads 9:56.

At least it's Saturday. *Thank God.* He doesn't have to go to school. Instead he gets to spend the afternoon with Emma—well, with her and the Lazarus Club. Dr. Beecher is taking them into Manhattan for an exhibit at the Metropolitan Museum of Art, which is fine with Jake, just as long as he gets to be around Emma.

Jake rubs his eyes, which sting from not sleeping for the past two nights. It feels good to rest, though. His body needs it. He lets his head sink more heavily into his pillow, and then he feels something on the sheets—something grainy and rough.

He pulls back the top cover.

Sand.

It's everywhere—alongside his hands and arms, stuck to the side of his stomach and legs. He can even feel grains between his fingers. Jake kicks off the rest of the sheet. Dark brown sand has hardened on his feet and toes. Part of the mattress around his heels is damp.

Jake practically jumps out of bed.

He steps away, still looking at the dirty sheets. Then he notices the sand already on the floor. The faint outline of footsteps from the door to his bed.

The Sea Cliff train station has only two tracks: one going west toward New York, the other continuing east to Oyster Bay. A faint smell of old tar and burnt matches comes from the tracks. You can even feel the weight of the train rumbling at your feet ten or fifteen seconds before it turns the tree-lined bend and pulls up to the station.

No one else from the Lazarus Club is at the station when Jake gets there. *This is a first,* he says to himself. Sure, he has never tried being early for anything in his life, but today is different. He hopes Emma will show up soon, so they'll have time to talk. He wants to tell her about his recent nightmares, about the fact that he was sleepwalking last night.

He needs to tell someone before he loses his mind.

He remembers how it all started—the meetings at Dr.

Beecher's place. The teacher had invited all of them to his house not long after they'd gotten back from New Orleans, not long after they'd made the decision to help Calliope and her daughter. . . .

After they followed Selene to the church cemetery, Caitlin ran off to get Dr. Beecher. Jake didn't like being alone with the girl. She was still holding on to that long knife, and she wouldn't stop staring at Reverend Michaels's body. Dirt covered his legs and chest. His hand stuck up from the soil like a dead rosebush, and the gash from his eye to his chin oozed with blood.

"No!"

The scream made Jake's heart skip. He turned around and saw someone running toward him. The ground was muddy and soft, and he felt as if he had sunk several inches. His legs couldn't move. Besides, there was nowhere to go. The figure got closer and closer. Jake tried to steady himself.

It was Calliope.

She rushed over to her daughter and swept her into her arms. The knife fell from her hands.

"What happened to my baby?" she asked, rocking Selene back and forth.

"Reverend Michaels," Jake muttered. "He's dead."

"My baby . . ."

Calliope was crying now. Hard, heavy tears. She moaned and clung to Selene, whose body was still stiff. Soon Emma, Duncan, and Lily came outside from the back door of the church. They must have heard Calliope, Jake figured. Before they could ask anything, Dr. Beecher and Caitlin hurried up the path. Everyone was standing around the grave and staring at Reverend Michaels now.

"What happened?" Emma asked.

"I don't know," Jake said. "Selene woke Caitlin and me, and she led us here."

"It's not her fault." Calliope stood up, her voice clear and sharp. "The old woman made her do it."

"What old woman?" Dr. Beecher asked, rubbing his thumb and index finger along his mustache. He wore sweatpants and a green Windbreaker. Jake had never seen him dressed so casually.

"The same one who caused the reverend to have those seizures. The same one who has been giving Selene nightmares." Calliope stepped forward. "It's because of what he did a long time ago. To her daughter."

Jake glanced at Caitlin. She stood close to Dr. Beecher, but instead of watching Calliope or looking at the reverend, she stared at Selene.

"I don't understand," Dr. Beecher said. "Reverend Michaels is dead—"

"Reverend Michaels was a bad man." Calliope's words were hard, angry. She was standing only inches from Dr. Beecher. Her eyes wide. "You have to help us. The police . . . they'll take her from me. Do you understand what I'm saying? They'll take her!"

"What are we supposed to do?"

"No one can know what happened." Calliope glanced at the grave holding Reverend Michaels's body. "My cousin Jonah. He can help. He owns an abattoir."

Dr. Beecher blinked several times, but his eyes never left Calliope's face.

Everyone was silent.

"What the hell is an abattoir?" Jake finally blurted out.

"A slaughterhouse," Dr. Beecher said. "She wants to get rid of the body."

"Some people deserve the bad things coming to them," Calliope continued. "Some don't. The reverend caused Abigail Dunn to hang herself from that there tree. Everyone round here knows it." She pauses to take a breath. "Her mama has been waiting a long time for this. She shouldn't have used my Selene—she's the same age Abigail was when the reverend started touching her, but that ain't no excuse to use Selene. Oristine will have to answer to Jesus for that."

Jake's head was spinning. Calliope's body swayed back and forth, and her hands gripped Selene's shoulders, as if she were afraid of falling over.

"We shouldn't have to pay for what the reverend done and for what Oristine did to my baby tonight. Help us . . . please. My cousin Jonah, he can take care of things."

Jake could feel the mosquitoes biting his neck and the thick air pressing down on him like a heavy coat. Then Dr. Beecher said something that surprised him.

"It's a decision we all have to make," he said. "Together."

So they stood in a circle by the grave. Jake thought about the things Reverend Michaels had done. "Some people deserve the bad things coming to them," Calliope said. "Some don't." Maybe that's true, Jake considered as he tried to imagine what would happen to Calliope if the police took her daughter and her new home away. He looked at the oak tree where Abigail had hung herself, and then he stared at Selene, whose clothes were still dark-wet with blood.

"We either call the police, or we make a promise never to tell

anyone what happened tonight," Dr. Beecher said, his head bowed forward as if he were about to pray. "We don't know what happened tonight," he continues. "We weren't here. Reverend Michaels was a sick man. Very sick. For all we know, he had another seizure."

Jake had a hard time believing that a twelve-year-old girl could kill the reverend—even if she did cut him with a knife. Something else must have caused it, Jake thought. Something that could be explained—not with voodoo dolls and sleepwalking but with facts. A seizure. That was the only thing that made sense.

"We came here to build a home for Calliope and her daughter," Dr. Beecher added. "To help them start a new life. Not to make things worse. We shouldn't take that away from them. Not after everything that's happened."

Jake could see Caitlin nodding in agreement.

"I promise never to tell," Caitlin announced.

"I promise," Dr. Beecher echoed.

And slowly, the rest of them followed.

"I promise."

"I promise."

"I promise."

"I promise."

But even after Jake said the words, he felt something burning inside his stomach. He looked in the grave one more time and saw the bloody gash running down Reverend Michaels's face.

Dr. Beecher nodded. "All of you go back to bed now. Calliope and I will take care of things from here."

Jake is standing at the edge of the Sea Cliff platform when he notices Duncan and Lily walking up the ramp. He wonders if he has ever seen them apart. Nope. He tries to picture them *together* together but can't. Not even a kiss. Duncan has geology, and Lily must have something too—something outside of herself, Jake figures. It's got to be outside, because she always looks like she's trying to run away from herself. Maybe not run away. She just wears her body like a winter coat in summer, as if it's something she can't wait to get out of.

"What do you want to come back as?" Duncan asks as soon as Jake is in earshot. The gel in his black hair makes it look as hard as granite.

"What are you talking about?" Jake looks at Lily, who shrugs.

"Reincarnation," Duncan answers, his hands tucked in his khaki trousers. "We were just talking about what we'd like to come back as. I said a white elephant in India because they're sacred and don't have to work."

"I want to come back as my cat, Periwinkle," Lily says.

"Your cat is named Periwinkle?" Jake asks.

She nods.

"Isn't that like a snail?"

"Yeah, but she doesn't move around very much. Arthritis."

"You see . . . ," Duncan begins, "she has a bit of a weight problem."

"Shut *up*," Lily says defensively but with a smile. "She's just fluffy."

Jake smiles. "Why do you want to come back as Periwinkle the cat?"

"My parents treat her better than they treat me."

There is something about her voice that makes Jake believe it. A sudden gust of wind chills him, and for the first time he notices a few clouds in the hazy sky. They remind him of wax paper. Thin and fragile.

"So . . ." Duncan turns to Jake. "What about you? What do you want to come back as?"

"I don't know. I've never thought about it."

"Well, what's the first thing that comes to mind?"

"Someone who doesn't dream," Jake says.

"What?" Duncan asks.

"Just kidding." But Jake can tell that Duncan doesn't buy it. His head tilts to the side, and he looks at Jake the same way he studies the paintings at Dr. Beecher's place—as something to figure out.

Duncan is about to speak again, but Jake cuts him off. "Look who's here," he says, pointing to Emma and Caitlin.

As they walk up the ramp, they couldn't look more different, Jake thinks. Emma's brown hair and quick stride, as if she's always ten minutes late for something. Caitlin's light blond hair, blue eyes, and bouncy walk. She waves and smiles as if they are all best friends, but outside of the Lazarus Club she doesn't hang with any of them.

The platform starts to rumble faintly, and Jake glances at his watch.

"It's early," he says to Duncan and Lily.

"Nope." Duncan corrects him. "This one is just passing through. Our train doesn't get here for another ten minutes." Then he calls out, "Hi, Em!"

"It's nice to see you, too," Caitlin responds sarcastically before Emma can speak. She wears dark blue jeans with a red top that almost matches her lipstick. Her black leather jacket seems new.

The thunderous rumbling of the train grows, and its horn screams twice as it comes into view. Jake feels a tug at his elbow from Lily.

"Isn't that Hickey?" she asks.

"What?"

"Hickey Stevens?"

Everyone hears Lily this time and looks. There he is, standing on the opposite platform. The bandage across his broken nose is bright white. It brings out the circular bruises under each eye.

"What the hell was Susann thinking?" Caitlin asks Emma. "I heard they never even hooked up."

"How should I know?" Emma replies, tugging at her white blouse and glancing at her feet.

"You're her tutor, right?"

"In English, not karate," Emma snaps.

"Check this out," Duncan interrupts.

Jake can't tell what Duncan is talking about at first; then he sees Susann Roberts hurrying onto the opposite platform. Hickey doesn't notice her. He has been watching the train speeding toward the station. Its headlight glowing. Its horn blaring.

"Susann!" Emma calls out, but her voice is swallowed by the noise of the train.

"She must want another shot at his nose," Duncan mutters.

Susann reaches Hickey a few seconds before the train races into the station. He doesn't see her stretched-out hands as they slam into his back and knock him off the platform in front of the train.

Swoosh.

In a flash of gray and silver, John "Hickey" Stevens is gone.

The train brakes with a piercing screech. The red light at the crossing still flashes steadily, and Susann stands on the platform. She doesn't look toward the train. She just stares at the spot where Hickey was standing a few seconds ago.

Jake turns to Emma. Her mouth is wide open. As he steps toward her, something on the track catches his eye.

It's the bright white bandage that was covering John's nose—lying across one of the iron rails, as if that were broken too.

8
LIVE AT FIVE

Karen McMillan from *Live at Five Eyewitness News* arrives a few minutes after the police. She is much shorter than she looks on television, Emma thinks, even with her shiny black heels. The man following her around seems to droop under the weight of the camera on his shoulder. He wears baggy jeans and a baseball cap, and you would pass him on the street without a second thought. He blends with things, which probably makes him a good cameraman, Emma figures. But Karen McMillan *Live at Five* doesn't blend at all. Her red dress, straight jet-black hair, perfect makeup, and well-practiced smile are as loud as a billboard.

And just as annoying.

Emma doesn't think there's much to smile about right now, but Karen McMillan has been beaming ever since she stepped out of the *Eyewitness News* van. She has talked to every cop in Sea Cliff, and they've spent so much time with her that you'd think *she* saw the whole thing.

As far as Emma can tell, Susann Roberts hasn't spoken since it happened. Emma ran to her as fast as she could—hurrying down the platform, crossing the tracks, and sprinting up the ramp toward the other platform. Jake followed, running too, but when they got there, Emma didn't know what to do.

"Susann, what happened?"

Susann didn't respond. She just stood with the stillness of a statue. Even when Emma grabbed her hands, which were icy and stiff, Susann only managed to blink. She wouldn't leave that spot—not until the police fastened handcuffs to her wrists and led her away, putting her in the back of a squad car. She is still sitting there, with her head lowered and her long, curly hair falling like a curtain over most of her face.

Karen McMillan approaches the car. An officer wearing inappropriately tight pants stands nearby and nods. Karen taps on the window with her microphone.

"Susann," she begins, her voice artificial and theatrical. "I'm Karen McMillan from *Live at Five Eyewitness News.* Could I ask you a few questions?"

Susann doesn't move.

"I just want to get your side of the story on record. For your own good." Karen pauses. "I understand," she continues, "that John Stevens was popular with other girls on the cheerleading squad. Is that why you did it?"

Officer Tight Pants approaches Karen and gently touches her elbow. "We have to take her to the station soon. Her parents have just been notified, and an officer is bringing them there . . ."

Emma can't hear what Officer Tight Pants says after that. She's not surprised though. His low, nasally voice was difficult to hear even when he stood right in front of her a few minutes ago.

Tight Pants: My name is Officer Miller, and I need to ask you a few questions. What did you see, exactly?

Emma: Not much. It happened really fast. The train

was coming into the station, and Hickey . . . John . . . he was gone.

Tight Pants: Your friends said that Susann Roberts ran toward the victim. Is that true?

Emma: Yes.

Tight Pants: So you saw that. Did she put her hands on him?

Emma: I'm not sure.

After that he ran his hands through his dark hair in frustration and stood a little straighter.

Tight Pants: Stay here. I'll be right back.

As he hurried down the ramp of the platform, Jake, who was sitting on the bench where Tight Pants had told the rest of them to wait, came over to Emma.

"Okay," Jake says, glancing at Tight Pants, "you've got a huge package. We get it."

Emma laughed, even though she wanted to cry and scream and run away all at the same time. Jake put his arms around her, and she felt calmer. He has a mellowness that rubs off on people, Emma has noticed. But it's not just being mellow. There is something kind about him. He knows when people need him, she thinks. He knows that she needs him.

He is still holding her now, and the hug feels good. She presses the side of her face into his chest, and his shirt smells like cedar. She inhales deeply. She isn't thinking about Hickey Stevens, though she can vividly picture the way the train seemed to swallow him up as it charged by the station. Emma is replaying her last tutoring session with Susann: the cheerful pink clothes, the teardrops on her notebook, and her story about sleepwalking. Emma imagines Susann getting out of bed, walking into the kitchen, and filling the sink—her body perfectly still until she dunks her head into the water and starts screaming. Emma wonders if a train rushing by sounds like a scream underwater.

"It's like what happened to Selene," Emma says into Jake's shirt.

"What?"

"Susann had been sleepwalking for days before she hit Hickey at school. And now this. You said Selene was like a zombie the night she woke you, right?"

Jake releases her and steps back, his hands sliding down her arms before letting go. "Kind of, yeah."

"So . . ." Emma drags out the word. "What if it's happening again?"

"You mean someone did this to her."

Emma nods.

"But why?" Jake asks.

"I don't know."

Emma can hear Jake take a deep breath as he lowers his head.

"What's wrong?" she asks.

"I . . . I have to tell you something."

Emma used to think that her heart wasn't much different from an eggshell: cracked from use and too fragile for most hands. She remembers her first kiss, under the weeping willow in Billy Wagner's backyard. He'd sat at the desk behind her for most of sixth grade without saying a word. Billy didn't talk to most folks, so it didn't really surprise Emma when he slipped her a note in class one day. Emma can still remember the words, because it was her first kind-of love letter. Also, it was short:

> If you like honeycomb, you should come over after school today. It's real sweet. And I'd like to share it with you.

So they ate honeycomb under the branches of that willow tree and kissed. She could taste the sugary sweetness on his tongue and feel his saliva on her chin. But after that he never asked her back, for honeycomb or anything else. Emma didn't understand why, but Billy wasn't much of a talker. So that was it—the first crack on the shell of her heart.

Then there was Bobby Lee Harper, who used the word "love" like most people use salt—adding it to everything without thinking. *I love my Xbox. I love skateboarding. I love you. I love barbeque sandwiches.* No, Bobby Lee wasn't very discriminating when it came to "love," but Emma had never heard those words from someone who kissed her with hard, impatient lips before.

At winter formal Bobby Lee went off to drink beer behind the auditorium with Hank "Lowlife" Digby and "Sleazy" Steve Boozer—which was his real last name, by the way. Emma thought Bobby Lee hung out with the two biggest losers in Elon, North Carolina, so she wasn't looking forward to going out back and telling Bobby Lee that she'd come to the dance to dance. But she did anyway.

And she found him there with Laura Mills—just the two of them, his hands on her breasts and her pink lipstick smeared on his neck.

Another crack.

Most eggshells break, and that's what happened to Emma's heart when Mom died.

She started to feel a dull pain in her chest as soon as Dad woke her up that morning. It was still dark outside and cold.

"Your ma wants to see you," he said from the doorway, and turned around. He didn't wait for Emma and Gwen to get up. He just left. His voice was flat as a tire, and he walked like someone with a hundred-pound bag of grain on his back.

But when Emma and Gwen got to Mom's bedside, she was already gone. Her face was sunken, and her arms appeared toothpick thin. There was a bandana where her hair used to be. Gwen kissed Mom's forehead, but Emma couldn't get that close. There would be no more good-byes and I-love-yous coming from her mom's mouth. Sure, Mom had been saying those things a lot, but Emma wanted to hear her voice one more time. Actually, that's not true. Emma wanted a hundred-thousand-million more I-love-yous.

She still does.

Emma is convinced that she heard a pop inside her chest right then and there: the shell of her heart shattering. It hurt to breathe, and she thought if she lifted up her shirt there would be a bruise or scar or something. A mark on the outside to show how bad it hurt inside.

But her pale white skin hadn't changed a bit.

After that, Emma figured that nothing—no one—in the world could glue the mess inside her chest back together.

Until Jake.

She is thinking all of these things as he stands in front of her, trying to tell her something.

"It's okay," Emma says, and she reaches for his hand.

Jake can hardly get another word out of his mouth before Officer Tight Pants and another cop shuffle up the ramp and announce that they need to take formal statements. The taller one, whose silver tag reads OFFICER ZIVAS, starts with Caitlin, Emma, and Lily. Tight Pants talks to Jake and Duncan.

Caitlin seems overeager to share, but that doesn't surprise Emma. Caitlin just likes attention. She likes sitting in the front of the class where everyone can see her. She likes the way men—from the guys at school to Officer Zivas—respond to her blond hair and raspy voice. She likes being one of the most popular girls at Saint Opportuna. But Emma imagines that the Caitlins of the world must be lonelier than most other people. Not because they need so much attention, but because the times without it must feel so empty to them.

"She didn't stop. She went right up to him and pushed . . . ," Caitlin continues, and Officer Zivas scribbles something on his notepad.

A car engine starts. From where Emma is standing, she can see Susann being driven away slowly, without sirens or flashing lights. Farther down the tracks police are still escorting people off the train and to the station, where buses wait to take them to another stop. And Karen McMillan *Live at Five* is interviewing some of the passengers—holding out her microphone and nodding sympathetically.

But the interviews stop as soon as a black van pulls up. It's the coroner. He has come for the body of Hickey Stevens, Emma assumes.

Immediately Karen McMillan *Live at Five* turns to the

cameraman and barks, "Roll!" Then she begins, the camera light shining brightly on her face.

"Good afternoon, this is Karen McMillan for *Live at Five Eyewitness News.* Tragedy has found its way again to the small town of Sea Cliff. John Stevens, a senior at Saint Opportuna High School, was found dead today—after being pushed in front of that train earlier." She points behind her.

Jake is now standing next to Emma, and everyone—the police officers, Caitlin, Lily, Duncan—is watching Karen McMillan *Live at Five*'s report. Except it's nowhere near five o'clock, Emma thinks as she glances at her watch. It never occurred to her that "live" news wasn't really live. Until the last few months it never occurred to her that so many things aren't what they seem to be.

"All of this only two days after a terrible car accident claimed the life of fellow student Jeremy Carson," Karen says into her microphone. "And I have just learned something else. A few hours ago another senior at Saint Opportuna, Jennifer Hagar, was reported missing by her parents. . . ."

9
WORDS

After Karen McMillan ends her report, Jake blurts out: "I have to go!"

Maybe he feels so edgy because he keeps replaying Jennifer Hagar's name over and over in his head and his entire body feels itchy, as if sand is sticking to his skin. Or maybe it's smelling the burnt tar of the train tracks and thinking of Hickey Stevens.

Either way Jake is sure of one thing. He can't hang around much longer without going insane or getting totally toked up. He needs time to think, to figure out what's going on. *Don't freak out,* he tells himself. *Stay calm.*

He turns away from the others and walks off the platform. He can hear his name being called, but he's not sure by whom. The air feels cooler now. Icy, almost. Jake tucks his hands into his pockets and quickens his pace. He only gets a few more steps before Emma is at his side.

Jake turns toward her and notices the way the neckline of her white blouse shimmers like glitter. He wants to talk, but words can have a way of making things worse sometimes. Once you say a thing, you can't take it back. Jake's father—who is a big believer in the power of clichés—says over and over, "Actions speak louder than words." But Jake doesn't buy it. Not for a second.

What if Emma hears about these terrible dreams and never wants to speak to him again? Could he blame her?

Jake looks at her, and his stomach knots.

He is quiet for a long time, and he knows that she is waiting for him to talk. He likes that about her—how she's okay with silence sometimes.

"I guess it started a few days ago," Jake begins. . . .

10
WARNINGS

After dinner that night Emma doesn't have to wait long before she can sneak out of the house. She sits at the edge of her bed with the door closed, thinking about her walk home with Jake. She keeps replaying his dream of killing Jennifer and his waking up to find sand in his bed. She can picture the way he stuffed his hands deep into his pockets when he talked. He hardly looked at Emma, as if he couldn't take the chance that she might judge him.

"Just because you walked in your sleep doesn't mean you hurt Jennifer," Emma said, but that didn't seem to help. When they got to her house, he told her good-bye and walked away fast, his hands still in his pockets.

She wanted . . . she wants those hands to touch her face and his mouth to kiss her deeply. She wants to feel the heat of his body pressing against hers, to feel his passion. It drives her crazy to think that he might still want Caitlin that way and not her. *Why won't he touch me like that?* Emma keeps asking herself.

She glances at the clock on her dresser: 7:59. Suddenly a series of chords rings out from the piano. With the first note of the Beethoven, Emma knows that her sister won't move for the next hour and that her dad has settled into his favorite chair near the piano, a book in hand.

Emma quietly makes her way downstairs and pauses in the foyer. From here she can only see the lower half of her dad's body—legs crossed and an open book in his lap. The shiny black body of the piano reflects a distorted, fun-house version of the room.

Emma darts into the kitchen, carefully unlocks the back door, and slips outside.

A cold wind is dragging pudgy clouds across the night sky. Still no rain, but from the chill Emma can tell a storm is coming. She didn't grab a jacket, but that's okay. She's not going far.

Ms. Martinique Dupré doesn't have a porch light, so her house is darker than the others in the neighborhood. She doesn't have much of a front yard, either, just a gravelly driveway that's big enough for only one car. Wooden shingles cover the house, and they make Emma think of a cabin—the kind of place you'd expect to find hidden in a forest, not on a street lined with houses. A faint red light glows through the curtained window by the front door.

Emma climbs the six steps leading to the door and is about to knock when it swings open.

"Is that you, Emma Montgomery?" Ms. Dupré asks, her words thick with a New Orleans drawl. She wears a loose yellow gown, and her body fills the entire door frame.

"Yes, ma'am," Emma replies, surprised at how quickly she slips back into southern mannerisms and expressions when she's around other people from the South. It's a nice feeling—like hanging out at home in your pajamas. Comfortable. Easy.

"What a pleasant surprise! Come in, come in." Ms. Dupré puts her arm around Emma's shoulders and leads her across the threshold.

Emma has never been inside this house before. Ms. Dupré

spends most evenings sitting on her back porch, sipping tea or some such thing and rocking back and forth in her swing. That's when she and Emma talk sometimes. Over the hedges that separate their backyards. Ms. Dupré in that swing. Emma standing on the lawn.

Ms. Dupré's living room reminds Emma of a church. It's dimly lit and cool, and it smells strongly of incense. A row of stained-glass windows hangs on the wall above the fireplace—each one with a different combination of red, blue, green, and yellow glass. A large cross, which appears to be made of bone, has been mounted on the far wall. Beneath it there is a red velvet couch and a coffee table with two silver candlesticks and an old tarot deck on it. In the corner stands a lamp with a colored shade, which gives everything a reddish hue.

"Please sit down," Ms. Dupré says as she leads Emma to the couch.

Emma eyes the cross warily and wonders if the two intersecting bones are human or animal. Something in the pit of her stomach gets fist tight, and she feels nervous all of a sudden, as if she shouldn't have come.

"Not to worry," Ms. Dupré explains, as if she can read Emma's mind about the cross; "it's just petrified wood. Please, have a seat."

She stands by the couch until Emma sits, then takes a place right next to her—their knees almost touching. The closeness makes Emma uneasy.

"To what do I owe the pleasure?" Ms. Dupré asks.

"I . . ." Now that she's here, Emma isn't sure where to begin. Even through the incense, the room smells of sweat. "I want to ask about Jake Hardale. You read his cards a few days ago, and—"

"That's a private matter," she says calmly.

"Well, he told me about it, and he's scared. He's been having these dreams, just like this other girl in town, and I thought . . . I thought you might have some idea how to stop them."

"Something is happening around here." Ms. Dupré leans closer to Emma, and her eyes appear black in the reddish light. "I think you should stay away from that boy."

"What?" Emma snaps.

"You heard me."

"But why?" Emma asks, feeling defensive and scared at the same time.

Ms. Dupré shakes her head.

"Tell me why," Emma insists.

"You know why," she begins in a whisper, almost as if she's talking to herself. "It's already inside him."

"What?"

"A force he can't control."

A pain starts to throb in Emma's forehead, and she feels dizzy. "There was this old woman in New Orleans—Oristine Dunn," Emma begins, her voice shaking. "She . . . she started hurting this man because of something terrible he'd done a long time ago. She was casting spells. Putting needles in dolls. Giving people nightmares that would make them do things." Emma inhales, and she can feel her heart racing. "She made this little girl sleepwalk, I think." The words spill out of Emma with relief. It feels good to tell someone who wasn't there. "Could the same thing be happening here?" Emma asks.

Ms. Dupré takes Emma's hands in her own. Her knuckles are thick and knotted, and she holds on to Emma tight. The room now seems smaller. The reddish light makes Emma feel as if she is trapped in a darkroom. "Magic is a powerful thing," says Ms. Dupré.

Emma tries to pull her hands away, but Ms. Dupré's grip tightens. "But I don't believe in any of that," Emma says quickly.

"Then why are you here?"

Emma shakes her head.

"I'll tell you why. You believe just enough. Maybe it's superstition or fear, I don't know, but it doesn't take much. You best be careful, or this magic . . . it'll come for you, too."

"Me?" Emma practically jumps up from the couch, wrenching her hands free. "You sent me that note! 'It's coming for you.' Those are your words, aren't they?"

Ms. Dupré leans forward, and her mouth opens slightly. Emma notices that one of her bottom front teeth is missing. "I just wanted to warn you."

"What's coming for me?" Emma demands.

"The nightmares, child."

Emma backs away to the door. She grabs the latch, but it won't budge. "I have to go," she says.

"Stay away from that boy, you hear? He's not safe!"

The latch pops up, and Emma pushes her way outside. She breathes in the air as if she has been underwater and scrambles down the steps. Drizzle moistens her face as she steps into the narrow, empty street. Once again she can hear Gwen practicing the Beethoven sonata, and the somber notes seem to linger with the misty rain.

Her heart races. Last week Emma would have called Ms. Martinique Dupré plum crazy. But after the things that have happened with Susann and Jake, she isn't so sure what to make of her. *Would Jake hurt me?* Emma asks herself. *Could he? No way. But Susann killed Hickey and—*

Emma wishes she could stop thinking altogether. She takes a few steps toward her house, when something emerges from the bushes there. The form is bulky and shapeless in the dark.

Emma freezes, not sure what to do. Two other shapes appear as well. They're beside the first one now. All of them are moving forward. The red light still glows in Ms. Dupré's front window, and Emma realizes that she needs to get back there. Fast. She tries to move, but her legs feel glued to the pavement.

"Emma," a strained voice calls out.

She finally takes a backward step away from the three figures.

"It's me," one of them says more urgently.

"Who?"

"Jake. I'm with Duncan and Lily," he adds.

"Jake?" Emma stops moving.

The figures get closer, and she can see that it really is them. Jake's black clothes blend into the darkness, and Lily's hunched shoulders make her seem menacing in the shadows. Duncan is skeleton thin.

"What are you doing here?" Emma asks.

"Duncan and Lily came to my house. He—" Jake turns to him.

"I've been having nightmares," Duncan says, tucking his hands in the pockets of his khaki pants. "Jake said something earlier about not wanting to dream, and I figured it must be happening to him, too."

"I told them about Susann's dreams," Jake interjects. "It can't be a coincidence. All of us dreaming like this, right? Not after New Orleans."

The rain falls in more solid drops now, like someone tapping your shoulder, and Jake glances up at it. Even a few feet away he smells of recently smoked pot—stale and smoky. Emma feels a pang of irritation.

"Is it the same dream over and over?" Emma asks.

"Mostly." Duncan's eyes widen as he speaks. "I'm walking down a street, and my body starts to catch fire. My fingers and arms always go first. Then my feet and legs. My face burns last." He takes a deep breath.

"He has been sleepwalking too," Lily adds softly.

Duncan nods.

"One morning he was standing outside my house," she continues, and then puts her hand on his shoulder. "He didn't wake up until I was right in front of him."

"Have you . . ." Emma hesitates, reluctant to go on, but she has to know something. "Have you ever dreamed of hurting someone?"

"What? No." Duncan turns to Jake. "Have you?"

Jake looks at Emma as if she just slapped him in the face.

"I'm sorry," she says. "I'm just trying to figure out the connection between you, Duncan, and Susann. There's got to be some reason you're all having nightmares and sleepwalking."

"What about Jeremy?" Lily asks, dropping her arm back to her side.

"What about him?" Duncan asks.

"What if he's another victim, like Hickey Stevens?"

"He was in a car accident," Jake snaps defensively.

Lily shrugs. The rain falls harder now.

"You think someone might have caused Jeremy to drive into that tree?" Emma pushes.

"Maybe," Lily responds, looking at the ground. "I still know his sister. I could ask her if anything strange was happening at home."

All of a sudden, the music coming from Emma's house stops. Gwen must be done practicing, which means Emma doesn't have much time to get back inside.

"Lily, try to find out more about Jeremy," Emma says, a little surprised to find herself taking the lead. She would have expected Duncan to be giving orders by now, but she can tell that his nightmares have left him shaken. "And we should ask around to see if anyone else at Saint Opportuna is sleepwalking."

"Okay, but what are we supposed to do until then?" Duncan asks, his face lined with worry.

"Don't sleep," Emma replies.

"Very funny," Jake mutters.

She turns to him. "I'm serious. Is there any place we can all crash tonight? We need to keep an eye on each other until we figure out what's causing this. My dad's a light sleeper, so we can't stay here."

"My parents can sleep though a war," Jake says. "They go to bed by ten."

Duncan looks at Lily, then Emma. He clasps his hands tightly in front of him. "I'm in."

"Me too," Lily says.

Jake nods. "Okay. Come over at eleven. There's a back door that leads to the laundry room. But . . ."

"But?" Emma asks.

"Well . . ."

"What?"

"How long are we supposed to keep this up?" he says, and his eyes appear dark as his clothes.

Emma glances back at Ms. Dupré's house, and in her mind she replays the woman's warning about Jake: *Stay away from that boy. He's not safe!* Emma doesn't believe it. She won't.

"As long as it takes," she says.

11
THE HOUSE OF ORISTINE DUNN

Jake doesn't expect Caitlin to show up, but there she is, standing in his backyard with the others when he opens the laundry-room door at eleven o'clock. Her olive cargo pants and tight white shirt remind him of New Orleans. It's an outfit she wore a lot last summer.

"Lily called me," she says as an explanation, and steps inside.

Jake hasn't been thinking about Caitlin at all. He has been thinking about what it would be like to spend the night with Emma, to lie on his bed together, to be with her in his room until dawn. He figured that Lily and Duncan would want to be together too, so there would be some privacy. But Caitlin changes things. After they all go to his room, Caitlin sits on Jake's bed, and he can see the irritation on Emma's face.

Duncan has brought a sleeping bag, and he immediately starts unrolling it on the floor. He wears the same clothes from earlier—a buttoned-up white dress shirt and khaki pants. It's what he always wears, Jake thinks, and he gets an image of Duncan's closet filled with rows of the same shirts and pants.

"I thought we weren't supposed to sleep," Caitlin says somewhat sarcastically as she points to the bag.

Duncan smiles weakly before dropping into a cross-legged

position on top of it. Then he stares at the shelves full of car parts, tools, and tin cans.

"I thought bookshelves were for books," Duncan says to Jake.

"My mother hates it too," Jake mumbles, not sure what to say as he watches Emma walk across the room and sit in the desk chair.

"Should we be drinking coffee or something to stay awake?" Lily asks as she steps over to Duncan. Her long brown dress reaches to her ankles, and she has to pull it up slightly to sit down.

"We could look at some online porn," Duncan says, and Lily hits his bicep. *"Owww."*

"I've often thought of starting my own porn website," Caitlin adds with a smile.

"That's a surprise," Emma mutters.

"What?"

"Nothing," Emma answers sharply. "I just thought you had a few already."

Caitlin's face tightens.

"I have some movies we can watch on my computer," Jake interjects nervously. They all need to stick together right now, he thinks. Not fight. He moves toward the desk where Emma is sitting. "Tons of movies, actually."

"Any porn?" Duncan asks, and Lily hits him again.

"This sleepover was *your* idea," Caitlin says sharply, staring at Emma. "Why don't you stop worrying about whether or not your boyfriend still has the hots for me and tell us how this is supposed to help. Huh?"

Jake can see Emma's face redden. "We're here to make sure no one sleepwalks."

"We can't babysit each other forever."

"That's why we have to figure out what's happening."

"And how are we going to do that?"

Emma lowers her eyes. A big part of her is afraid that they might not be able to stop it, and she wonders if everyone in the room can see the fear on her face. But that's not all. She's afraid of the possibility that she might start having nightmares too. Like Jake and Duncan and Susann. "I'm not sure."

"I don't understand something," Lily says, and she brushes her reddish-brown hair out of her eyes. "Calliope said that the old woman, Oristine Dunn, caused Selene to sleepwalk, but how? I mean, we never saw her do anything."

Caitlin scoots farther back onto Jake's bed until the pillows are directly behind her. "I did."

"What?" Jake says.

"Yeah. You were there too."

Oristine Dunn looked like the oldest woman alive, Caitlin thought. Her face was as wrinkled as the bottom of your feet after sitting in the bathtub for hours, and she had no teeth. None that Caitlin could see, at least.

Oristine lived in half a house. The other half had been swept away in the floods after Katrina, but she still lived there anyway—even though the police kept trying to make her move. Half the living room, part of the dining room (including the table), one bedroom, and the bathroom sink—gone. Oristine was one of the few people who stayed behind in the neighborhood where Habitat was building new houses. She didn't want a new house, though. She stayed to keep an eye on Reverend Michaels.

That's what Calliope had said.

After Caitlin found the voodoo doll and saw the names Phobetor, Morpheus, and Phantasos written in blood, she'd asked Calliope about the reverend.

"He grew up here, right around the corner from the church," she'd said. "I guess folks thought he was born to be a preacher. Until the rumors started."

Reverend Michaels ran an after-school program at the church. Tutoring kids in math and English and teaching them about Jesus. Oristine Dunn's little girl, Abigail, was one of the kids who came to the church a lot. Sometimes she stayed later than the others, but that wasn't a surprise. Everyone knew Abigail wasn't so bright.

She started having nightmares about three years later. Sometimes she dreamed that her body was turning into a tree. Her chest hardening into bark. Her arms becoming branches and her hair becoming leaves. Other times she saw white feathers between her legs, and the head of a swan appeared there.

Oristine had her suspicions about these nightmares, long before Abigail could talk about the way Reverend Michaels touched her. Oristine was never quite right after that—thinking about the reverend and her baby girl. Abigail was never quite right after that either, Calliope explained. She had to retake ninth grade, and on her sixteenth birthday she hung herself from the large oak tree behind the church.

Oristine kept watch over Reverend Michaels after that. Why she waited so long to put a curse on him and cast spells, Calliope wasn't sure. "It ain't my business," she told Caitlin. "And it sure as hell ain't yours!"

So one afternoon Caitlin dragged Jake to Oristine's half house. Caitlin knocked on the front door several times, but no one answered. So they walked to the side with the missing walls. It reminded Caitlin of the dollhouses she'd played with as a kid—the way you could see into every room. No privacy. No secrets.

From the yard Caitlin and Jake looked into the living room. There were old chairs with purple upholstery, and a blue couch covered in plastic. Oristine sat in a rocking chair with an old book in her hands. The reading lamp next to her was on, even though there was plenty of light from the midday sun.

"This must be yours," Caitlin said as she stepped inside; she held out the voodoo doll she'd found at Calliope's house.

"Mine had pins in it." The old woman continued rocking. She didn't look at Caitlin or Jake. "I don't recall inviting anyone into my home."

"I just . . . How do you do it?"

Jake turned toward Caitlin. "What the hell?" he whispered.

"Do what?" Oristine asked.

"Cast spells."

"Ahh, I see . . ." Oristine stood up. Her shriveled face was yellow like parchment. She wore a loose light-blue summer dress. "The white kids want to play magic."

Oristine put her book on the table next to the rocking chair, and she picked up a cigarette and a silver lighter. Caitlin and Jake watched as Oristine lifted the flame of the lighter to the cigarette between her lips. It flickered and went out.

"Boy," she said, facing Jake. "Do you know what Job said about nightmares?"

Jake shook his head. A new flame shot up from Oristine's lighter, and she held it in front of her for a few seconds. Again the flame disappeared before touching the tip of her cigarette.

"He said: 'When I say, My bed shall comfort me, my couch shall ease my complaints; Then thou scarest me with dreams, and terrifiest me through visions: So that my soul chooseth strangling, and death rather than my life.'"

Oristine's lighter burned again. This time it touched her cigarette, which glowed orange-red. She held it there for a long time.

"Boy, do you know what Job said about fear?"

Jake shook his head. Once again he watched the flame of the lighter rise and fall.

"'For the thing which I greatly feared is come upon me, and that which I was afraid of is come unto me. I was not in safety, neither had I rest, neither was I quiet; yet trouble came.'"

The flame seemed to shake and vibrate more rapidly now.

"Boy," Oristine said, "wrap your arms around this girl and squeeze the air right out of her."

Jake stepped behind Caitlin, and before she could react, his forearms were tight around her arms and across her stomach.

The fire from Oristine's lighter vanished and appeared again. "Harder," she commanded.

Caitlin tried to break free. She kicked and tried to yell out, but Jake's arms were crushing her. She struggled to breathe.

"Jake," Caitlin cried, "you're hurting me!"

His grip got stronger.

"Perhaps," Oristine said to Caitlin as her lighter snapped off, "we should cover your mouth?"

"No." Caitlin started twisting from side to side, anything to break free. Oristine smiled and watched.

"Enough!" she yelled suddenly, and Jake let go.

Caitlin collapsed to the floor, coughing, and Jake—he just stood there, his hands at his sides, and his eyes locked on the silver lighter in Oristine's hand.

"Now get out of my damn house!" Oristine said to both of them. She sat in her rocking chair again and picked up the book. "And don't come back."

"How do you do it?" Caitlin pressed, still trying to catch her breath. Her hands shook with fear. "What's the secret?"

"You don't deserve no answers," Oristine said without looking up from her book. "Get away from here."

"That's bullshit!" Jake says as soon as Caitlin stops talking.

"You don't remember going to her house?"

"Kind of, but none of that happened," Jake said, noticing the shock on everyone's face. Even Emma's.

"What happened, then?" Caitlin asks.

Jake thinks about it, but nothing comes to mind. Not the missing walls. Not the rocking chair. He can't tell if he was really there. "I don't remember exactly. I mean . . . it was a while ago."

"She did something to you, just like she did to Selene," Caitlin explains, lowering her eyes. "So I went back to see her after that."

"What?" Jake asks. "Are you crazy?"

"You almost *killed* me, Jake," Caitlin snaps. "You almost killed me, and she made you do it—with nothing more than a lighter and some words. Think about that. I mean . . . I wanted to know how."

"What did she say?" Emma's words seem to startle her, as if Caitlin were in some kind of trance.

Caitlin shakes her head. "Just what we already know—that Selene was the same age as Abigail when it began, when the reverend started to abuse her."

"You think," Lily begins, "that what Oristine did to Jake is happening here?"

Caitlin shrugs.

Jake can feel Emma watching him, but he doesn't look at her. He knows that she's wondering if he hurt Jennifer.

"But why?" Jake snaps. "What did we do?"

"You know what we did," Duncan says flatly. "We're all guilty."

"Of what?"

"Silence," Duncan replies.

"What about Jeremy and Susann?" Lily protests. "They had nothing to do with Reverend Michaels."

"Maybe it doesn't have to do with the reverend," Emma says, still looking at Jake. "Maybe it's something else—something else we have in common."

"Like what?" Caitlin asks, her voice less aggressive than before.

Emma shakes her head.

"Even if that's true," Duncan says, "it doesn't tell us who is doing this. I mean, it can't be Oristine again . . . can it?"

No one speaks for a while after that. Jake can't make sense of it. None of them can. Did he really try to hurt Caitlin at Oristine's house? How could he not remember? Soon the room is so quiet that they can hear the faint sound of cicadas outside.

"Maybe we should just watch a movie . . . ," Duncan says.

For a long time they munch on chips, drink the Red Bull that Duncan brought, watch B movies, play video games, and talk. Well, Jake doesn't talk much after Caitlin's story, but he listens to her and Duncan and Lily. Emma is pretty quiet too.

Eventually they decide to take turns staying awake. Duncan volunteers for the first shift. He'll watch them sleep and make sure no one starts walking. Then it'll be Caitlin's turn, then Jake's. Each of them agrees to stay up for about two hours, "unless you know you're going to fall asleep no matter what," Emma adds.

Duncan turns out the lights.

Emma and Jake lie on his bed under the comforter. Caitlin has borrowed Jake's sleeping bag, and Lily crawls into Duncan's. Duncan sits in the corner with his iPod. The light from the screen occasionally makes his face glow.

Jake is nervous about touching Emma with so many people around. She rolls toward him, and he can feel her hand on his waist. He tries to move closer to her body without making any noise, but the bed creaks. *Damn.* He hesitates. Her face is so close that he can feel her breath.

A sleeping bag rustles, and Jake wonders if Caitlin is rolling onto her side—away from them. He kisses Emma. Deeply. Her leg slips between his, and he slides his right hand beneath her shirt. He cups her breast, and she leans forward, pressing her upper body against his. Her lips tickle his neck now, kissing and dampening his skin. Jake's left arm feels trapped beneath his own body, but he doesn't want to move.

The swooshing sound of a sleeping bag fills the room again.

Emma must feel Jake stiffen because she pulls back. He can't see her eyes in the dark and wonders if she is going to say something. Instead she kisses him on the mouth. Then her hand slides slowly down his chest and stomach. She doesn't slip it inside his jeans. She just presses it against his erection.

Jake inhales sharply, and he's pretty sure he hears Duncan mutter, "Get a room."

Jake isn't sure what time it is when he gets up to go to the bathroom, but when he opens the door, he sees Caitlin standing by the sink in front of the mirror.

"Duncan fell asleep early," she says, still studying her reflection.

"What time is it?" he asks.

She shrugs. "Remember those nights in New Orleans? Just us sleeping on the floor of Calliope's house?" Caitlin steps over to him. "Remember when we used to be that way?"

Jake's legs feel heavy. Yes, he remembers every minute, but all those memories have been colored by hurt and anger. There was a time when he would have given anything to hear these kinds of words from Caitlin—words to know that she missed him, that she still wanted him. But not anymore.

"Did that really happen?" he asks.

She blinks, startled. "What do you mean?"

"That thing at Oristine's house." His voice is hoarse. "Did she make me try to hurt you?"

Caitlin nods. "Maybe it was already inside you and she just knew how to let it out."

"What do you mean?"

"Like a genie in a bottle." Caitlin pauses, tracing her finger down the center of his chest. "Maybe you always wanted to hurt me, Jake." Caitlin pulls her hand away from him. "Good night."

She squeezes past Jake and returns to her post as sentinel.

Everyone left at five thirty in the morning, to get home before their parents would notice. After they slipped out the back door, Jake dragged himself into the kitchen for a bowl of cereal. He is still thinking about Emma and the way she touched him. He wants to think about that and nothing else, but he can't get Caitlin's words out of his head: *Maybe you always wanted to hurt me, Jake.*

Now it's 5:33.

He reaches for the cabinet and turns on the small black-and-white television underneath. As the screen brightens, Jake sees Karen McMillan *Live at Five* standing on the beach by the old boathouse—the boathouse in his dream.

"The body of Jennifer Hagar, a seventeen-year-old student at Saint Opportuna High, was found right here late last night, near Tappen Beach. According to a spokesperson for the police department, she was reported missing by her parents yesterday." Karen McMillan pauses. A gust of wind has blown some of her hair into her face, and she brushes it aside.

"The Hagar family told police that their daughter left home Friday afternoon to go to a friend's house for the night, but she never arrived. They didn't discover this until Saturday morning.

"Preliminary forensic reports suggest that Jennifer died

shortly after she went missing. The condition of the body, which was submerged for approximately thirty-six hours, will make determining the exact cause of death difficult, police said. But she doesn't appear to have been molested.

"Police believe that Jennifer was killed on shore and pushed into the water. The current, which has been particularly strong due to recent storms, pulled her body into an old fishing net that held her underwater. A fisherman noticed the body and contacted police.

"When I asked Officer Rod Miller if the police had any suspects or any explanation for the rash of teenage deaths in Sea Cliff, he refused to comment. This is Karen McMillan—"

Jake hits the television, and the screen goes black. A pain surges through his temple. He moans and grabs onto the countertop. Damn. The headache reminds him of swallowing a cold drink too fast on a hot day. His entire head buzzes.

After last night Jake wonders what good these slumber parties are going to do. They don't have much time to figure out what's causing the nightmares. At some point he's going to fall asleep without anyone else around. At home? In class? Then what? Will he have another dream of killing someone? Will he actually do it? Will he crush someone with his arms? Emma?

The kitchen door suddenly rattles from a series of knocks. Jake opens it and finds Officer Tight Pants and two other cops standing there.

"Jake Hardale," Officer Tight Pants begins, "are your parents home?"

"Yeah. Why?"

"We'd like their consent to ask you a few questions."

"Me?" Jake can feel his throat tighten. "Questions about what?"

"About the murders of Jeremy Carson and Jennifer Hagar."

Jake wouldn't recommend jail to anyone. Ever. The holding cell smells strongly of disinfectant, which makes him wonder what needed cleaning so bad. There is one bunk bed against the far wall, and in the corner there's a nasty-looking toilet without a seat. The fluorescent lights overhead buzz with the insistence of flies.

A bulky figure lies on the bottom bunk. A thick gray-black beard swallows up most of his face, and his brown skin is deeply pitted and lined. Jake is worried about waking up Rip Van Winkle as he climbs up top. *Out of sight, out of mind,* he hopes, using another cliché from his father's vast repertoire.

The white lights pulse steadily, and the brightness—in this room without windows and clocks—makes the entire place seem timeless. It could be two in the morning or twelve noon.

His stomach suddenly jumps into his chest, as if he's standing in a quickly falling elevator. Jake grabs onto the mattress for support.

I'm in jail, he says to himself. *They think I killed Jeremy and Jennifer!*

He wants to scream and cry and puke at the same time. The piercing pain in his head returns. *Calm down,* he tells himself. *Jeremy was in a car accident. You didn't have anything to do with it. Not a thing. And you've never met Jennifer. Why would you hurt her? It's all a mistake.*

He closes his eyes, but he can't block out the whiteness of

the light. It seems to push through his eyelids. Bright. Burning. Relentless. Each fluorescent tube hums loudly.

"Younger than most," a voice from below grumbles.

Jake freezes, not sure what to do.

"I said . . . ," the man in the bottom bunk repeats, louder this time, "you're younger than most criminals, heh?"

The bed squeaks as the man swings his feet onto the floor and stands. His face—with that gray-black beard, matching hair, and translucent blue eyes—is only inches away now. Jake's heart beats machine-gun fast. He wants to back away, to push up against the wall, but he's too afraid to move.

The man gazes up at the lights.

"'Darkness visible.' That's what this place is, heh?"

He smiles, and the egg-yoke color of his teeth makes Jake's stomach turn.

"That's from *Paradise Lost.* 'Darkness visible.' How many bums you know can quote shit like that?" he asks.

Jake can feel his lips move, but no sound comes out.

"Well? I asked you a question." The man's smile dries up, and he leans closer to Jake. His body smells of rotten vegetables.

"One, I guess," Jake manages to say.

"Told ya." The man nods.

The cell door clangs as Officer Tight Pants pulls it open. Jake almost wets himself with joy. He never thought he'd be so happy to see a cop.

"Leave the kid alone, Harvey," he commands, and the bearded man shrugs before plopping back down on the mattress.

"Come on," Officer Tight Pants says to Jake. "You're with me."

The interrogation room has the same institutional flair as a typical high school. White walls, a crappy table, cheap iron-colored chairs, and no windows. When Officer Tight Pants brings Jake inside, a large man wearing a white shirt and an electric-blue tie is sitting at the table. A uniformed officer stands behind him in the corner. He stares at something on the floor, so Jake can't see his face.

"Where are my parents?" Jake asks, surprised that they're not in the room.

"I've asked them to wait in the lobby," Officer Tight Pants replies.

"But I want to see them now!"

"Later." The officer's voice is tight and percussive. "This is your lawyer, though. Mr. Maximilian Forrest."

"I'd like some time to confer with my client, Officer Miller." The lawyer's voice is as big as his body, too big for the smallness of the room, Jake thinks. He folds his hands in front of him on the desk, and his fingers remind Jake of sausage links.

"I just want to ask Jake a few questions. The sooner we get this over with, the better," Officer Tight Pants Miller replies, sitting down across from Jake and Mr. Forrest. There is a bulky file in front of him, but he doesn't open it.

The lawyer nods. "It's okay," he says to Jake, who wants to scream, *What the hell are you talking about? Nothing's okay!*

"Did you know Jeremy Carson?" Tight Pants begins, holding himself perfectly still.

"A little. We had some classes together in tenth grade."

He nods and then fires off a series of questions. Fast. Dry. His voice flat, and his eyes fixed on Jake's.

TP: When was the last time you saw him?

Jake: Last week, I guess. He brought his car into the shop. There was a small hole in his radiator, and I—

TP: So you worked on his car?

Jake: Yes.

TP: The radiator?

Jake: Yes.

TP: You didn't work on the brakes?

Jake: There wasn't anything wrong with his brakes.

TP: How do you know that?

Jake: Well, he didn't say anything about them.

TP: The brake line of his car was cut that afternoon, Jake. Do you understand what that means? Jeremy's death wasn't an accident.

Jake: But that's easy to miss if you're not looking for it!

Jake looks at Mr. Forrest, who smiles as if they're talking about the weather. *But a serious leak in the line . . . I should have noticed something,* Jake says to himself. *The chemical smell of the fluid. Stains on the inside of the tire. I was baked, sure, but still. I should have caught that.*

"Are you ready to tell me the truth now? Why did Jeremy really come to the shop that day?" Officer Tight Pants seems to relax a bit with this question.

"His radiator—"

"Frank," Officer Tight Pants calls out to the cop in the corner, "why don't you bring some of Jake's property in here?"

Officer Frank leaves the room quickly. He glances at Jake

on his way out; one eye is severely bloodshot.

A few seconds later he returns. In his hands is the smoking gun, Jake realizes. The bloody glove. The eyewitness video.

Officer Frank is holding Jake's Big Box of Pot—words that Jake actually wrote on the side of that shoe box one night while he was high.

"Where did you get that?" Jake asks angrily.

"In your bedroom closet. Underneath a tackle box and a Victoria's Secret catalog," Officer Frank says with a smirk.

Damn, Jake thinks.

"The judge issued a search warrant before we picked you up this morning," Officer Tight Pants explains as he takes the box from Frank and places it on the table in front of Jake. "As you can see, there's enough pot in here to get the entire island high for a month. That makes you a dealer, in my book. And do you know what happens to drug dealers? Prison. And I'm not talking some cozy holding cell either."

The room starts to spin, but at least he's talking about drugs, not murder, Jake thinks with some relief. Still, his dreams keep flashing in front of him. What if he's responsible? What if he is acting out his dreams—like Susann and Selene must have? Maybe it wasn't motor oil drowning him. Maybe it was brake fluid that had become contaminated.

"It's time to tell the truth," Officer Tight Pants continues calmly. "Why did you cut that brake line?"

"I didn't—"

"Enough." Mr. Forrest's booming voice shakes the table. "Mr. Hardale is a juvenile, and he has never been arrested for drug possession. So I don't care if he has ten Big Boxes of Pot in his underwear. Without proof of intent to sell, you can't charge him with anything other than possession, and I'll have him home within the hour."

Mr. Forrest unfolds his sausage fingers and leans back in the chair.

"As for this brake-line business," he continues, "you can charge him with murder right now, or this interview is finished."

"What about this?" Officer Tight Pants opens the bulky file. Inside, there is a plastic evidence bag with a pink cell phone in it.

"What?" Jake replies.

"We found this in the alley behind Island Auto Repair—where you work," he says. "Where you sell drugs."

"So—"

"So, it's Jennifer Hagar's phone. Would you like to tell me how it got there?"

"How the hell would I know?" Jake snaps.

"Officer Miller," Mr. Forrest interrupts. "This is circumstantial evidence at best. Anyone, including Jennifer, could have left that phone there. Now if you don't have anything else—"

"I'm just trying to give this young man a chance to come clean." Officer Tight Pants puts his hand on Jake's Big Box of Pot. "Perhaps she was there just buying some pot, right?"

An image of Jennifer facedown on the beach flashes in front of Jake. Then a vision of Jeremy pumping the brakes and slamming into an oak tree. Then his arms wrapped around Caitlin, squeezing. And then he sees Rembrandt's Lazarus rising from the dead. All coming at him like a slide show.

"I . . ."

"You don't have to say anything." Mr. Forrest puts his hand on Jake's shoulder.

"I . . ."

"It's not a good idea to talk," Mr. Forrest advises. "This interview is over."

"I want to know what happened to Susann," Jake spits out.

"Excuse me?" Officer Tight Pants replies.

"Susann Roberts. What happened to her?"

Officer Tight Pants studies Jake's face for a moment before answering. "She has been remanded to a psychiatric facility until her trial. Frank"—he glances at the other officer—"take him back to the holding cell."

With that, Jake is led back to jail by Officer Frank. Mr. Forrest walks alongside them. His grasshopper-thin legs seem moments away from collapsing underneath the weight of his massive torso.

"It shouldn't take too long to process the paperwork," Mr. Forrest says. "So hang tight."

"Thank you." Jake looks up at his round, reddish face.

"Don't thank me. Thank your parents. They hired me."

They continue down the rest of the corridor in silence until Jake is put back into the cell. It's empty. There's no Harvey to quote *Paradise Lost* now. The only sound comes from those damn buzzing white lights—white lights that make minutes feel like hours and hours like days.

Jake sits on one of the lower bunks and covers his face with his hands. Just maybe he'll wake up at any second, and all of this—Jeremy, Jennifer, Selene, Reverend Michaels, the nightmares—will have just been a terrible dream.

SUNDAY

12
WORDS NOT TO FORGET

Emma has never spent much alone time with Lily Ambrose. Not that Emma has anything against her. Quite the opposite. There is something genuine and kind about Lily. Sure, she doesn't say a lot. She tends to nod after people finish talking, and that's that. *How are you?* Nod. *What did you think of that test?* Nod. *What are the first six digits of pi?* Nod. Lily treats words like some people treat fancy clothes or expensive jewelry—something to be saved for special occasions. But you can always tell that Lily is listening for real, and that's a rare thing, Emma thinks.

But today Lily is talking a lot.

"I like used bookstores the best," she says, as if Emma asked her a question.

"Really," Emma responds halfheartedly—not because she doesn't care. She is just exhausted from staying up so late. She got home before Dad and Gwen woke up, but during breakfast he asked, "Have you been sleeping okay?" Emma felt her chest tighten in panic. *Does he know?* she thought. *No way.* Her dad isn't the passive-aggressive type. He would've been waiting up and calling her friends and God-knows-what-else all night if he had known she was gone. "You sure?" he asked, and Emma nodded.

". . . and those kinds of novels especially," Lily adds enthusiastically.

Emma has no idea what Lily's talking about, but she nods anyway. "Uh-huh," she adds for good measure.

Emma doesn't want to hear any more about used books right now. She wants to know where Jake is. He hasn't responded to her calls and texts all day. She checked Island Auto and even went to his house, but no one was there. What if he fell asleep? she has been wondering. They're all tired. They're supposed to stick together. Her stomach feels tight—with worry and with thoughts about being in bed with him last night. About kissing him. About feeling his hands on her stomach and breasts. About hearing the way his breath changed when she touched him. . . .

"Used books are like these living things, you know," Lily continues. "They have a history, a life of their own. I mean, even the name scribbled inside the cover can tell you things about a person. If she was hurried or careful? If she preferred a nickname? You can learn a lot from what someone underlines, too—if she was reading this book when she fell in love or after she just had her heart broken."

Emma nods. "Hey, where's Duncan? I didn't think you guys went anywhere without each other," she says.

Lily smiles. "He said he was going to talk to somebody about his nightmares."

"He found someone else who's having them?"

"I'm not sure."

"Is he coming to the meeting?" Emma asked, and the question reminds her of Dr. Beecher's phone call telling her to come over today. "We should talk about what's been happening and get some work done on your senior project," he said. "I'll expect you at five."

"Yeah, he'll be there." Lily smiles again as they turn the corner onto Dr. Beecher's street.

Emma has noticed that about Lily. Even hearing Duncan's name makes her giddy. Her plain clothes and slouched shoulders seem to disappear, and she smiles. Emma feels a pang of jealousy. It's not that Jake doesn't still make the back of her neck tingly. He does. He has a quiet intensity that pulls her close like a magnet. The way he sometimes gets lost in his own thoughts. The way he can feel close and faraway at the same time. But Emma worries about how these nightmares—and the terrible things happening in town—have come between them, about how they have changed them.

"Anyway," Lily continues, "I bought this used book last week, and the person wrote all sorts of things in the front. Mostly lists. Groceries to buy. Bills to pay. That kind of thing. But one list was kind of strange." Lily pauses.

A list lover, Emma thinks: a person after her own heart.

"Yeah?"

"It was called 'Words Not to Forget.'" Lily brushes some of the hair from her face.

"What did it say?"

"Nothing," Lily replies. "There were no entries. I guess she never got around to that one."

"I guess not."

Emma tries to come up with her own list of words not to forget, but she can't imagine forgetting the ones that are really important to her. Maybe "desiderata." Her Dad used it once to describe his feelings for Mom. "I knew as soon as I met her," he said a few days after her cancer was diagnosed. "Desiderata—what is desired and what is required. That's what she is for me. Desiderata."

Emma wonders if her heart will feel the same way about Jake one day.

Dr. Beecher's yellow house towers above the others on Prospect Street. The arched windows remind her of a medieval castle, and the spires on his roof look as if they could poke holes through the thick clouds overhead.

"When you called, you said you had something to tell me about Jeremy," Emma presses. They don't have much time before they get to Dr. Beecher's front door.

"Not exactly," Lily replies, as if she wishes they could continue talking about used books forever. "His sister, Amy, said something about Terrence Mallory."

"Terry?"

"Yeah."

"The witch?"

"Yeah."

"What does he have to do with anything?"

Lily nods. "Well, a couple nights before the accident, Terry was standing in the Carsons' driveway—leaning against his car, smoking. So Jeremy went outside to talk to him, but Terry wouldn't say anything. Not a word. He just kept smoking. It really weirded Jeremy out."

Lily stops talking as they get to Dr. Beecher's front gate. Her shoulders curl forward again.

"Doesn't Terry live right around the corner from here?" Emma asks.

"Yeah, I think so. On Locust Street. The house with the 'No Pooping' sign."

"What?"

"You know . . . one of those signs with a drawing of a dog about to take a dump."

"Lovely." Emma checks her watch. "We still have some time. Why don't we pay Terry and his 'No Pooping' sign a little visit?"

Terrence Mallory is a witch. Not the kind with a broomstick and cauldron and curly black hair. He is a senior at Saint Opportuna who likes swear words and writing poetry about naked girls with big breasts. But he is also a self-proclaimed practitioner of Wicca. Terrence doesn't say much in Dr. Beecher's class, but Emma has heard him talk about witches in theology, which everyone is required to take before graduating. Usually Steven Carter or some other ogre on the football team will start it. They'll yell out "devil worshipper" or something equally original, and Father Mike will say, "Ho, ho, ho . . . we'll have none of that here." Then Terrence spouts a few things about Wicca as a religion that celebrates nature and the four elements and blah, blah, blah.

That's when Father Mike stops the discussion.

Terrence's bedroom in the Mallory house doesn't look very much like a witch's den, Emma thinks. Not unless there's a coven of witches somewhere that celebrates Xbox, the *Sports Illustrated* swimsuit edition, and saxophones. But then again Emma doesn't know much about Wicca.

"What the hell are you doing here?" Terry asks as soon as they enter. He holds a tenor sax in both hands. His short, sandy-blond hair looks wildly mussed up, as if he just dried it super fast with a towel.

"Your mom said you were home," Lily offers as a kind of explanation.

Terry blinks several times. "Let's try this again. What the hell are you doing here? I mean, we've talked like once, maybe twice, ever, and now you're in my house. What's that all about?"

"We wanted to ask you about Jeremy," Emma begins. "You knew him, right?"

"Kind of."

"You went to see him the night before he died," Emma says.

Terry smiles.

"Right?"

"You sound like a cop."

Emma turns to Lily, but she is staring intently at the floor.

"Lily used to be friends with Jeremy and Amy, his sister," she continues. "Anyway, Amy mentioned that you came over that night, but she wasn't sure why."

"It's not like I was invited to dinner. That punk ass wanted to borrow some money."

"Money?"

"Yeah, that paper stuff you buy things with." Terry adjusts the saxophone in his hands, and Emma fights the urge to hit him over the head with it.

"He was rich," Emma says flatly.

"He wanted to score some shit from Jake, but Mommy and Daddy were holding back on his allowance for some reason."

"Did you give it to him?"

"Yeah, which totally blows, because now I'm out three hundred bucks." Terry scratches his forehead.

"Sorry you're so broken up about his death."

Terry either doesn't notice Emma's sarcasm or doesn't care. "Is that the end of the interrogation, officer?" he asks. "Because unless you're both here to pleasure me, I really need to practice."

Emma is ready to storm out of there, but Lily blurts out. "Do you do magic?"

"What?"

"You're a practicing witch—at least that's what you tell everyone," Lily coaxes, and once again Emma is surprised by her today. "So do you cast spells or what?"

"My religion is none of your business," Terry replies, but his voice is strained and less confident.

"What about sleepwalking? Can you make people do that?" Lily pushes.

"Get out," he snaps.

Lily doesn't flinch. "We'll pay you to show us how."

Terry lowers his head as if he's considering it.

"I said get out . . . now!"

His face turns bright red this time. He takes a few steps toward them, and after they back out of his room, he slams the door.

"Out!" he yells again.

Emma leads Lily downstairs fast. Mrs. Mallory is sitting in the living room with a puzzled expression on her face.

Emma and Lily hurry outside.

"What was that all about?" Emma asks, somewhat out of breath.

"I'm not sure," Lily says, "but that guy is a real ass."

"He knows something."

"'You sound like a cop,'" Lily mimics, and they both laugh. "So what do we do now?"

"Well, if he is casting spells or something, there's only one person in town he'd go to for help."

"Who?"

"My neighbor."

Emma dreads the idea of seeing Ms. Dupré again. She has always liked Ms. Dupré, but being inside her house the other night really frightened her.

"Come on," Emma adds. "We're going to be late."

13
420

For almost an hour in the lobby of the police station Jake's parents speak with Mr. Forrest about their son the drug dealer and accused murderer.

"He's a first-time offender, so if they charge him with possession of marijuana, he'll most likely be placed on probation with a period of home confinement," Mr. Forrest explains loudly enough for the entire town to hear. "Right now they want to question him about the deaths of those two kids. They may just be fishing for information. It's too early to tell."

"Oh, God," his mother mutters, and Jake expects her to have a heart attack right there. "I've always heard that marijuana is a gateway drug."

"To *murder*?" his father snaps.

After that no one speaks. They get into Jake's father's white 2008 Acura TSX, which still smells like new leather, and they begin what promises to be the longest one-mile drive in Jake's life. As his dad drives, Jake can see the whiteness of his knuckles on the steering wheel. Gripping. Releasing. Gripping again. Maybe he is imagining what he will do to his son's neck once they get home, Jake wonders. His mother stares vacantly out the passenger window.

At each stop sign he expects his father to explode—yell, turn bright red, spout a few clichés for good measure. That kind of thing. Sure, his father has never been the screaming-yelling type. He prefers stern looks and sarcastic barbs. But if any day is going to test the man's breaking point, this is it.

Instead nothing happens. Nada. Zilch. The Big Zero. Jake isn't sure which is worse: another speech about Jake the Son of Great Disappointment or complete silence.

He's starting to think he'd prefer the speech.

After they pull into the driveway, Jake goes quietly to his room. *Maybe they're planning to give me up for adoption. I'm sure some family out there wants a homicidal drug dealer for a son,* Jake thinks as he checks out his room.

The cops picked up his stash all right. Jake's Big Box of Pot. His pipes. His bong. All of it has been confiscated. They even took his computer.

Damn.

Jake is prepared for the pot, at least. He always figured his mom would find something incriminating in his room one day, so he's hidden a few emergency doobies in the picture frame on his desk—behind the glass, along the bottom.

Jake picks up the photograph of his mother, father, and him in the garden courtyard of the Mission San Luis Obispo in California. Colorful rows of tulips and irises hug the path, and an arcade runs along the edge of the garden. It is supported by brick pillars. This trip was part of his dad's Summer of Family Fun three years ago, which should have been called How to Torture Your Only Son or Ruining a Perfectly Good Summer or Oh, My God, This Can't Be Happening to Me. Anyway, the "vacation" started in San Diego, and they drove up Highway 101, visiting all twenty-one California missions.

It took forever and a day, as his dad likes to say, and Jake lost count of the number of times he considered throwing himself from the moving car. But when the engine overheated outside of Solvang and the tow truck took more than an hour to get there, Jake finally lost it.

"Most normal people come to California to see the Hollywood sign or to go to the beach," Jake blurted out. "But not the Hardales. No, we visit the twenty-one most boring places in the state!"

His father was leaning against the trunk, watching the cars on the highway. "Look at all these people driving by," he said to Jake. "Most of them have probably never visited a mission or thought about the history of this state."

"So?"

"I know it doesn't matter to you now, but you'll remember this trip. You'll remember it more than playing video games and skateboarding. That's the thing about history. You can try to drive past it, but it's always with you. It makes you who you are. Just like family."

Whatever, Jake wanted to say, but he knew better than to mouth off when his dad got pseudophilosophical. The conversation was over anyway. The tow truck pulled up, and soon they were crammed in the front seat with the driver, on their way to San Luis Obispo.

It's true, Jake has to admit: He hasn't forgotten the trip. But if his dad is right, what does Jake's history say about him? About who he became after that trip to New Orleans?

Jake can feel another headache building. He turns over the picture frame, removes the back, and finds two tightly rolled joints there.

Praise the Lord.

"Hello?" Emma calls out.

No one answers. Emma is about to speak again when she hears a murmur. A faint noise or whispering seems to be coming from the hallway.

"Hello?"

Still no answer.

Dr. Beecher has never showed them any other part of the house, so Emma is nervous about following the sound. She approaches the vine-carved handrail of the staircase by the front door. A corridor starts here that appears to run to the back of the house. Its towering walls must extend all the way up to the roof, Emma figures, but she can't be sure. They disappear into the dark rafters overhead.

At the far end of the hall she can see a slightly opened door. The murmuring seems to be coming from there. A light flickers from inside, but it isn't strong enough to reach much beyond the frame.

Emma starts down the hall, running her fingers along both walls. The texture reminds her of a damp sponge. She doesn't want to keep touching them, but she is afraid of letting go, of stumbling over something in the dark. Emma can hear Lily shuffling closely behind her.

Now the sound is getting clearer. It's a voice: Dr. Beecher's.

"James Braid is considered the father of hypnosis," he explains. "He even coined the term. It's derived from the name of the Greek god of sleep, Hypnos—but you already knew that."

"Do you believe in that stuff?" another voice asks. "Hypnotizing people?"

"I do," Dr. Beecher responds. "Think about the ways that society tries to hypnotize us all the time: telling us what to buy, what to wear, how to act. Images—powerful images—come through your television sets and your computer screens. And what do most of us do? Nothing. We sit down and absorb them passively. We can be so unaware of the messages behind what we're really seeing."

Emma reaches the door. From here she can see partway into an office. A tapestry covers most of one wall. The red, brown, blue, and black fabric has faded, leaving only the outline of a scene. An emaciated horse drinks water from a stream; his rider, a knight in armor, has fallen to the earth, and blood is spilling from the wound in his neck. A raven perches in a nearby tree. Waiting.

As Emma knocks, the door swings inward. She can see Duncan standing next to a desk. He holds two books in his hands. Dr. Beecher leans back in a throne-sized leather chair. A green handkerchief peeks out of the vest pocket of his white suit. As Emma and Lily enter, he removes the round glasses from his face and starts cleaning them with a cloth.

"Welcome," Dr. Beecher says with a smile. "Duncan and I were just talking about some books."

Duncan nods, still looking down at one of them: *Franz Mesmer and the Origins of Hypnotism.*

"I got here early and saw these books in the living room," he says, and Emma notices his bloodshot eyes and mussed-up hair. His head bows slightly forward. He looks tired, and it reminds her of her own fatigue.

"I thought I had another volume on mesmerism back here,

but I don't seem to be able to find it." Dr. Beecher puts the glasses back on the bridge of his nose. He shuffles through some papers on his desk, and one of them catches his attention.

"You know . . . ," he begins softly, holding the paper in his hands, "I've been trying to find out about some of my former students recently. Where they are. What they've made of themselves. And do you know what I've learned?" He pauses but doesn't wait for an answer. "One of them is in a California jail for grand theft auto. Another became a lobbyist for big tobacco. And one girl seems to be building a career off a humiliating experience on *American Idol* last year—"

"*American Idol*?" Emma blurts out, trying to hold back a laugh.

"Yes, it's a reality show where young people sing or something like that," Dr. Beecher explains, as if she and the rest of the world might not have heard of it. "So I've been asking myself," he continues, "if this is what I have to show for it, what's the point?" Dr. Beecher blinks several times, and there is a dejected expression on his face.

"If this is what you have to show for what?" Emma asks.

"For being a teacher." His voice is flat, and Emma can see a faraway look in his eyes. Duncan still stares at the book in his lap. "In New Orleans I saw something in all of you, though. Something special. You have such promise." Dr. Beecher smiles and looks around at each of them. "Perhaps, we should—"

"Si—" Caitlin steps into the room and stops abruptly. Her mouth drops open as she looks around the office. Duncan. Lily. Emma. She takes all of them in with a mixture of hurt and anger on her face. "What are you doing?"

"We were just heading up front to start the meeting," Dr. Beecher says as he gets out of his chair and moves toward the door. "We have to choose several more photos of New Orleans for your group project—"

"But I thought . . ." Caitlin hesitates. "I didn't know anyone else came back here, that's all."

Caitlin hasn't moved since coming into the office. A black skirt reaches just below her knees, and she wears a tight green top. Emma catches a whiff of lavender perfume.

"We were looking for some books," Dr. Beecher explains, as he ushers them out of the office.

Duncan and Lily step into the hallway first. Emma follows. As she glances over her shoulder, she sees Dr. Beecher put his hand on Caitlin's back to lead her out. Caitlin stiffens.

Lily sits on the couch, and a light seems to go off inside when Duncan chooses the chair farthest away from her. His face still droops with exhaustion, and he doesn't make eye contact with anyone. Emma plops down next to Lily.

Caitlin isn't in her usual place either. She keeps her distance from Dr. Beecher, sitting sideways in a chair with her legs over one of the armrests. Her bubbly enthusiasm for everything to do with Beecher has dried up, and Emma has to admit that she finds this Caitlin far less annoying.

Stacks of black and white photos have been placed on the table in front of them. Emma picks up a pile and flips through images of the French Quarter, the St. Charles streetcar, and Calliope and Selene's house at different stages of building: the frame, Duncan and Lily painting the living room, all of them standing in front of the completed home.

As a group they have to put together a PowerPoint presentation of the trip. Each of them is writing about a different part of the slide show. Most of the photos have been chosen, but they still need a few more. Emma isn't sure that any of them really know what to say about the images. How can they look at Selene and not think of what happened to Reverend Michaels? Dr. Beecher keeps offering suggestions, but Emma needs to find her own words—to make sense of it for herself.

She looks at the entryway. No Jake. She keeps hoping he'll stroll through the door, his long arms dangling by his sides and a totally mellow expression on his face. Typical Jake. The sinking fear comes back to her in waves. What if he fell asleep today and had another nightmare? Emma considers checking her phone for a text, but she doesn't want to risk offending Dr. Beecher. Not tonight. His face is less animated than usual, and his white suit appears dirty in the yellow candlelight. He checks his watch.

"Still no Mr. Hardale," Dr. Beecher mutters. "I left a message for him at home, but I'm not sure if he got it. Well, let's give him a few more minutes." Dr. Beecher looks out at the group. "Perhaps we should talk about a painting or two before we work on the slide show. To warm up. Caitlin?"

Caitlin gets up sluggishly and walks over to the projector in the corner. She seems to struggle with the carousel at first. It clicks several times before locking into place. A few seconds later the machine starts to hum. A white light flashes on the screen above the fireplace. Then there's another flash, and the first painting appears.

A beautiful woman with a sword saws through the neck of a man lying in bed. Blood sprays onto the white pillow and sheets. His muscular arms are taut, struggling to push himself up. His mouth is wide open, frozen in one final, agonizing yell. Beside the woman, a handmaiden holds a sack for his head. Her face is deeply wrinkled with ferocity.

"Here Caravaggio is telling the biblical story of Judith, who beheaded the general Holofernes in order to save the Israelites from the Assyrian army," Dr. Beecher explains. "What details surprise you about this painting?"

Silence. Even Caitlin holds back her usual eager-beaver commentary.

Bang.

Everyone jumps, including Duncan, who seems to have nodded off. One of the books has slipped off his lap onto the floor.

"Now we're awake," Dr. Beecher says with a strained smile. "So, Duncan, what do you think?"

Duncan blinks several times as he studies the painting. Judith's unflinching determination. Holofernes's blood. The handmaiden's meanness.

"I . . ." Duncan glances at Lily. "I'm sorry. I have to go."

With that, Duncan gets up and runs out of the house.

MONDAY

15
BLAZED

if u r home come out. need to c u.

Jake reads the message on his phone a few times before getting out of bed. It's from Emma. He glances at the clock: 12:17 a.m. *That can't be right,* he thinks as he wipes the crumbs off his shirt and looks at the explosion of cookie fragments on his comforter. He remembers pulling apart a few dozen Double Stuf Oreos and licking the icing centers before eating the rest, but that was a while ago. A couple hours, maybe.

He must have fallen asleep. That means he didn't dream. Not at all. For the first time in days, he feels relieved.

Jake heads downstairs and slips out the kitchen door. The wind outside is crisp and a bit rough. He should have worn a jacket, he thinks. As he gets toward the front of the house, he hears someone whisper his name.

"Jake?"

It's Emma, lingering at the end of the driveway behind some hedges. She waves. Someone else is with her. Probably Lily.

"I've been calling and texting all day!" Emma snaps. "We need to keep an eye on each other tonight. Where the hell have you been?"

She and Lily step into the driveway as he hurries up to them. Lily's glasses are slightly fogged, but unlike usual she seems antsy, shifting her weight from one foot to the other.

"Jail."

"What?"

"The cops took me away while I was eating a bowl of Lucky Charms," he says.

"What?" Emma's eyes widen in surprise. Her hair is pulled back, and she is wearing all black as well. Jeans and a black leather jacket.

"For killing Jeremy and Jennifer. It's okay right now. The cops took all my weed, though. Well, most of it." He pauses. "Hey, we match."

"What?"

"Our outfits."

"Jesus." Emma steps back. "Are you high?"

"Well . . ." Jake hesitates, surprised by her anger.

"Come on," Lily interjects. "We don't have time for this."

"Look," Jake begins, "it has been a pretty bad day. I mean, my parents haven't talked since they bailed me out, and I'm tired of thinking about all the shit that has been happening, you know. So—"

"So you got blazed," Emma snaps.

"Blazed? Well I don't think that's what the kids are calling it today, but—"

"Lily just got a weird e-mail from Duncan," Emma says, cutting him off and handing him a folded piece of paper. "He said he has to do something tonight that can't be helped."

Jake reads the printout of the e-mail: *Lil, I'm sorry. The nightmares are getting worse. Of me burning. Of me in your house. Of you burning too. I can't go through with it. I have to do something.* Jake looks up at Lily and Emma. A dull fear makes the skin on his neck and arms feel cold.

"I talked to him a few times after the meeting tonight, and

he seemed okay," Lily says, brushing the hair away from her face. "We were planning to come over here again tonight, but about an hour ago he wouldn't answer his phone or anything."

Jake feels somewhat light-headed. He leans back against the tree and closes his eyes. He has a sudden craving for something salty. Pringles, he thinks. Or Doritos.

"What does this note mean?" he asks.

Lily shrugs.

"I don't know," Emma says. "But we're going over to his house."

Jake looks at Emma. Even in the dark he can see the delicate whiteness of her face, and he has the sudden urge to kiss her, to feel something other than fear.

"I'll come too," Jake offers.

Emma looks down. "You don't have any shoes on."

"What? Oh . . . that's cool."

She shakes her head. "Come on. We have to hurry."

16
THE PROMISE

Emma is pissed. She has been worried about Jake all day. *All* day. Waiting for a call or a text or an e-mail. Hoping that he was thinking about her, missing her. Even a little bit. How could he *not* be thinking of her? Instead he was thinking about himself. Getting high and not considering her feelings for one second. He should have called after he got home from the police station. Period. Just to let her know he was okay.

Emma knows she's not being completely fair. He's scared. He's connected to Jeremy's and Jennifer's deaths somehow. And like the rest of them he's carrying around the memory of what happened in New Orleans.

"Ouch," Jake mutters.

He is a few steps behind Emma and Lily now, struggling to keep up. His bare feet are slapping against the pavement. The ground here is uneven and littered with loose gravel.

The rectangular shape of the Boyce house reminds Emma of two squashed pizza boxes, one on top of the other. Instead of cardboard, long strips of gray-green aluminum siding line the exterior. There is no sidewalk here, so the front door is practically on the street. One side of the house has just enough room for a carport that dead-ends into the hillside. The other side has a path that leads around the house at a steep incline.

"Now what?" Jake asks, breathing heavily.

Lily has already sent another text message to Duncan, so she tries calling. It goes immediately to voice mail.

"His phone is off."

"Well, it's like one in the morning," Jake mutters.

"Let's go around back," Lily says.

"What?"

"His room faces the yard."

Lily doesn't wait for either of them to say anything else before taking the path. Emma follows, and Jake stays close behind her. The stone steps aren't evenly spaced apart, and most of the time her foot falls in between them. To her left the bushes—crowded with leaves and sharp branches—seem to push toward the house, as if they want to get inside.

She bumps into a windowsill and stops, trying to get her bearings. Jake runs into her.

"Sorry," he mutters. "I can't see a damn thing."

"Shhhh," Emma whispers.

His body is only inches away from hers. She can hear his breathing, but the rest of him—his clothes, even his face—has disappeared into the darkness. Then she feels his hand squeezing hers. Her heart starts beating jackrabbit fast.

Clang.

The noise startles Emma, and she lets go. A few feet in front of her Lily has stopped moving as well. The initial percussive sound is followed by a scraping noise. Rolling or grinding. It's close, too, she realizes. Around back.

"Come on," Lily says.

They continue their climb along the side of the house and into the backyard. It's brighter here, but not from any light. It has something to do with the open space and the white cement of the empty swimming pool. A tarp has been left on the lawn like a crumpled paper ball.

A faint sound—like the grinding together of stones—is coming from inside the pool. Lily glances at Emma and Jake. Her face is tight with worry. No one speaks. They approach the edge together, taking slow, cautious steps.

As they get close enough to see into the pool, something moves below. Emma freezes, her heart still pounding like a drum.

Another sound comes from the pool now. Scraping and grinding again, but it's much softer than before. Suddenly, a light glows from the center, right above the drain. The small flame casts a faint circle of gold around someone who is kneeling. Head bowed forward. Hands shaking.

"Hello?" Emma asks.

The figure looks up.

"Get away," he hisses.

"Duncan?" Lily blurts out. "What are you doing?"

The flame from the lighter wobbles in his hand. He doesn't respond, but now Emma can see his wet clothes. What she thinks must be water drips from his face and hair. His shoulders bob up and down as if he's trying to stop himself from sobbing.

"You're not safe," he says to Lily, his voice shaking along with his hands.

"What are you—," Emma begins, but then she sees a can of acetone near the ledge of the pool. The label reads ACETONE. DANGEROUS—FLAMMABLE. He must have doused himself with that, she realizes.

"Jesus, Duncan, put down the lighter!"

"Come on, man," Jake says. "It'll be okay, just—"

"You don't understand. I . . ." Duncan shakes his head violently. "I won't be able to stop myself. Like Selene and Susann. There's no other way."

"Duncan, please," Lily begs. Her words crack as if she's about to cry.

But before she can say anything else, Duncan touches the flame to his chest, and his entire body ignites into a bright, roaring fire.

17
WHITE ELEPHANTS

Bluish-yellow and orange flames engulf Duncan's body. Hungry and mean. It happens so fast, Jake thinks. Duncan is burning to death right in front of him. The fire gets fiercer with his screams.

It takes Jake a few moments to realize that Emma and Lily are no longer by his side. Lily has grabbed the tarp and is trying to pull it toward the pool, perhaps to smother the flames. But it's too heavy. She drags it a few feet, then trips, falling on her side.

Emma is running toward the Boyce house, yelling "Help!" and "Fire!" Before she gets to the back door, one of the lights downstairs snaps on, and Mr. Boyce runs outside with a fire extinguisher. His T-shirt and boxer shorts seem too small for his pudgy, short body, as if he has thrown on his son's clothes by accident.

Jake is way ahead of him now. His legs seem to carry him forward as he jumps into the pool. The heat hits him in a wave. Solid. Forceful. Jake sees several puddles of rainwater on the uneven surface of the pool. Still water reflecting the yellow flames. He pulls off his shirt and charges toward Duncan. His eyes closed and the shirt out in front of him. Something to smother part of the fire.

Jake tackles Duncan, knocking him back and driving him into one of the puddles. For a moment the burning light surrounds Jake. He can see the brightness through his closed eyes. Then it's gone.

A hissing sound fills his ears. Spray from the extinguisher quickly covers Jake and Duncan with a thick, white goo that snuffs out the flames. Jake rolls to the side, but Duncan doesn't move. His skin is black and blistered and lined with red blood. The hair has burned completely off his scalp, leaving pink and purple-white strips of skin.

That's when the smell reaches Jake, when he really breathes it in. He turns his head and vomits.

This is the story he tells Officer Tight Pants, who is sitting next to him in the backseat of a squad car now, staring straight ahead while Jake speaks.

"Why were you here in the first place?" he asks.

"Duncan sent Lily a weird e-mail."

Officer Tight Pants clears his throat. "By weird do you mean suicidal?"

"Kind of, I guess."

"So your friend is suicidal, and instead of calling the police or Duncan's parents, you decide to walk over to his house in the middle of the night?"

Jake is silent.

"I don't need to tell you how bad this looks. This is the third death that you've been a part of somehow. *Third.*" He leans forward with these words. His unshaven face looks steel-wool rough, and it gives him a meanness Jake hasn't seen before.

"I tried to save him," Jake pleads, and his voice breaks. He is trying not to cry—not in front of this jerk. But he can still hear

Duncan's screams, just like he can hear Jennifer's muffled cries. Jake presses his hands over his ears. Anything to make it stop, to feel like he's not going crazy.

"Yes, you did," Officer Tight Pants admits softly as he opens the door. The dome light overhead flickers at first. "The paramedics say you're fine. They say you're damn lucky that Mr. Boyce's fire extinguisher worked." He gets out of the car and starts to close the door, then stops. "One more thing," he says. "Why do you think he did it? Why light himself on fire? I mean, if you're going to kill yourself, there has to be an easier way, right?"

But Officer Tight Pants doesn't understand, Jake thinks. It's about having dreams you can't escape. It's about not being able to stop yourself. Duncan wanted to escape. Period.

"Well?" Officer Tight Pants presses.

"Once," Jake says, "he told me he'd like to come back as a white elephant in India."

Officer Tight Pants stares at him for a moment, but Jake didn't mean it as a smart-ass comment. It's true. "Officer Zivas is going to take you home," he says. With that, Officer Tight Pants slams the door, and the light overhead goes out.

The wooden steps creak underneath his feet. One. Two. Three. To his left a swing wide enough for two sways back and forth as if someone were sitting there. It groans under an invisible weight.

The front door gives off the only color in the dark. Red. He tries the brass knob, but it won't turn. The door itself feels sticky like flypaper.

He pushes.

It swings open into a foyer crowded with bookshelves. A staircase with vines for handrails winds up to the second floor. He pulls his hands free, but something still covers them—something thick and moist.

Blood.

He steps into the living room. Candles burn on the circular table, and their light catches on the blade of a letter opener there. Wax drips on stacks of yellow parchment and unopened envelopes.

An antique chair has been knocked over. That's where she is—lying on the floor next to it. Her dark hair splays away from her head like an open fan. Blood is on the floor by her nose, and he can see a brown birthmark on her cheek.

He picks up the letter opener with his sticky hands. He grips the handle, then drops to his knee, plunging it deep into her chest—

"Emma!" Jake yells.

He looks around. A shelf filled with tools and auto parts. Computer desk with no computer. His NASCAR calendar. He is in his room but not lying in bed. He is kneeling on his floor with his hands in front of him as if he has just stabbed someone.

Jake stands, his hands shaking. He remembers being driven home. His parents had gotten a call from the police, and they were waiting in the living room for him. His mother had a faded terrycloth bathrobe wrapped tightly around her body, and his father wore a T-shirt and pajama pants. At least this time his father spoke:

"We'll talk in the morning, young man."

It was better than silence, Jake thought.

He went to his room. Sitting down at his desk, he pushed aside his physics book, folded his arms on the desktop, and buried his head in them. Then he wept. He cried like a baby, actually. Everything that had happened in the last few days seemed to pour out of him through tears and snot and blubbering. It felt good.

After that he must have fallen asleep and dreamed.

He didn't dream about drowning Jennifer or about Susann pushing Hickey in front of the train or about Duncan burning to death. No. He dreamed of killing Emma, the girl he is falling in love with.

He dreamed of killing her in Dr. Beecher's house.

TUESDAY

THE PRESENT DAY . . .

18
IN MEMORIAM

The howling leads her to this spot—the spot where she drives the shovel into the ground. The earth doesn't want to give way at first. It's thick with tree roots and weeds and decaying leaves. But she keeps digging feverishly. Breaking through. Going deeper. Soon the air smells of moist soil.

The sound beneath her gets louder with each scoop of dirt, and it starts to hurt her ears. She backs away from the hole—

Crack.

She has stepped on something. A pair of glasses with black frames. She is about to pick them up, when a coughing fit seizes her. Hard, deep coughs that shake her entire body.

She starts digging again, and the howling intensifies. She needs to get to the source of it, she tells herself. She needs to find out what it wants.

A new coughing fit grips her. This time she feels as if she is going to be sick. Her body tenses, and something erupts from her stomach up through her throat. She covers her mouth as it spills out.

Her hands fill. Not with liquid, but with dirt. Thick clumps of dirt.

Emma sits at the kitchen table now, her leg shaking nervously as she stares at the morning paper: MEMORIAL SERVICE FOR SAINT OPPORTUNA STUDENTS. The cover story only mentions Jeremy, John, and Jennifer, but Emma wonders if anyone at school knows about Duncan yet. If he'll be mentioned at the mass today.

Chilling memories of her nightmare flash before her. Digging faster and faster. The glasses crunching beneath her foot. A tightness seizes her chest now, and the kitchen starts to spin. Too much has happened in the last six days, she thinks. She needs to focus on something to stay calm, to keep herself from bursting into tears. Anything. The paper.

> A number of student blogs are claiming that Susann Roberts, the girl who pushed John Stevens in front of a train last Saturday, was suffering from a severe sleep disorder. Other students at Saint Opportuna High School are reporting their own experiences with sleepwalking and night terrors.
>
> Neither the Roberts family nor the school psychologist would comment.
>
> According to Professor Jonathan Riggs, director of the University Sleep Center at NYU, these behaviors are not uncommon in children and teens. "We would label what some of these students are experiencing 'parasomnias'—a sleep disorder that includes nightmares, sleepwalking, and even violent behavior while sleeping. In other words, a parasomnia is a condition where someone is acting out his or her dreams."

Emma stops reading. The article might explain what is happening but not why. Not who. Someone is causing this.

Emma doesn't remember falling asleep, exactly. Last night the police drove her home, and her dad made her sit at the kitchen table until she explained every detail. He looked worried and tired and old, like he did during those last few months with Mom. Emma doesn't know what time she dragged herself upstairs and collapsed in bed, her eyes burning with exhaustion and dry from so many tears. She has a vague memory of the howling sound—the sound that somehow dragged her out of bed. It coaxed her outside. That's where her father found her. In the backyard with a shovel in her hands.

He sits in the living room right now with his friend Dr. Feldman, who came over early this morning.

"She's sleepwalking . . . like the others," her dad whispers, and she can hear Dr. Feldman saying something about Ms. Dupré and voodoo.

The kitchen feels hot all of a sudden. Scorching hot. Sweat beads on her forehead, and another wave of dizziness hits her. Emma thinks of Duncan again and has to fight off the tears. She wishes her mom were sitting next to her, rubbing Emma's back with the palm of her hand. Her mom would make things better somehow.

But even her mom wouldn't have been able to change the fact that Emma is sleepwalking like the others. This can only mean one thing.

Someone else is going to die soon, she tells herself. *Someone else will die, and I'll be responsible.*

The school chapel at Saint Opportuna is almost full. The midmorning sun pours through the stained-glass window depicting Christ's temptation on the mountaintop. He wears a thick robe of red and white, and he gazes down at Satan, whose brown face and deep blue wings seem menacing. Pointing at the clouds beneath them, the Devil tries to persuade Christ to throw himself off the summit.

On the altar there is a table with four candles and four pictures: Jeremy dressed as Henry Higgins from the school's production of *My Fair Lady*, John in his basketball uniform, Jennifer in a formal evening gown, and Duncan's yearbook picture from junior year. His neatly parted hair and the shirt buttoned at his neck make Emma wince. It's too hard to see that photo and not remember the way his face looked last night—twisted in pain as the fire crawled up his skin.

She turns away and scans the pews for Jake and Lily. No luck. She remembers seeing Jake jump into the pool last night—throwing himself against Duncan, trying to save him. Her heart got fist tight. The thought of losing Jake was too much. It made her entire body feel heavy like lead.

Emma decides to slip into the first empty seat, right under Christ's stained-glass eyes. A few seconds later Caitlin squeezes in next to her and smiles. She wears a black dress that stops at her knees and does little to hide her flat chest.

It is surprisingly quiet for a room filled with two hundred teenagers, Emma observes. She can hear some sniffling and whispers, but almost everyone—even the teachers sitting in the front row—seems uncomfortably still. Shaken. Emma looks at the pictures again. Four pictures. Four dead students. How many more will there be, she wonders with a sinking feeling in her stomach. Are she and Jake next?

Emma swallows the saliva in her mouth, and it feels grainy like dirt.

The side door of the chapel opens, letting in a flash of bright sunlight. Dr. Beecher enters. No colorful handkerchief sticks out of his breast pocket today. He doesn't smile or wink at anyone. He just plods over to a place on the faculty pew. As he sits down, Emma notices Terry the witch a few rows behind him. He has turned partway around and is looking at her. His face has none of the meanness from the other day. His short blond hair is still a mess, but his blue eyes seem watery—whether it's from sadness or fear, Emma can't tell.

"What a freak," Caitlin mutters, glancing at Terry. Her hands fidget in her lap.

"He's not much for small talk, either," Emma replies.

"What?"

"Nothing." She looks back at Caitlin, who is concentrating on the photos. "Are you okay?"

"What do you mean?"

"You seem jumpy, that's all."

She stops moving her hands. "I hate these things—ever since my brother died."

"Your brother? I'm sorry . . . I didn't know."

Caitlin shrugs.

"What happened?" Emma asks, tentatively.

"My family moved here from Boston five years ago," she begins, turning toward Emma. "Right after it happened. Brian had lupus, but we didn't know it for a long time. He was ten."

"Lupus? I've heard of it, but I don't know—"

"It's a disease that makes your own immune system attack your body," Caitlin says, as if she has recited this fact a thousand times. Her hands fidget again. "Basically, your body destroys itself."

Emma can't help thinking about Duncan—about how his own dreams destroyed him. Emma can see the moment before he lit himself on fire. The way the lighter wobbled in front of him. It makes her think of Caitlin's story about Oristine Dunn, too—about the lighter she held before Jake. Is this what will happen to Emma next? Will she destroy her own body? Light it on fire? Bury herself alive? She starts to feel dizzy again.

"I'm sorry," Emma says. "I know how . . . I mean, I have an idea what that's like—losing someone." Emma knows that she is rambling, but she can feel her eyes stinging with tears. "My mom died. It was hard."

So here she is, opening up to Caitlin Harris of all people. Emma wanted to say something to show that she understands but instead, she looks like an idiot. A doofus. A total dork. Crying in front of Caitlin—Caitlin with the perfect smile and skinny body.

"I guess Dad wanted Brian more than me," Caitlin says dryly. She doesn't seem to notice Emma wiping away her tears. "After that he was angry most of the time. I tried to make up for Brian not being around, but it didn't change things. I couldn't do anything right. Not for him at least."

She looks up, and her eyes focus on Dr. Beecher.

Emma isn't sure what to say next. This is the longest conversation she's ever had with Caitlin. But once again the image of Duncan's lighter flashes before her. "We were there last night when Duncan died," Emma says.

Caitlin nods. "I heard." Her voice is no louder than a whisper.

Suddenly, a bell signals the start of the memorial service,

and both Emma and Caitlin jump slightly. The sacristy door opens, and Father Mike walks to the podium. The flowing white robe and purple vestment mask some of the roundness of his body. He carries a thick Bible with gold lettering and a bright red cover.

Emma looks around for Jake again but doesn't see him. The chapel is quiet until Father Mike opens the Bible and starts to speak. Emma closes her eyes, trying to block out everything—the sound of his voice, her nightmare, her theories about what's happening . . . everything—so she can concentrate.

So she can try to find a way to say good-bye to Duncan.

19

A BOX OF MATCHES

Jake has been sitting in the back of the chapel, avoiding Emma. He just doesn't know what else to do. Ever since his dream last night, he has been afraid—afraid of what might happen to her if he falls asleep again. How can he tell her about that? How can he look into her eyes and *not* tell her? But that's not the worst part.

The worst part is that he doesn't think he can protect Emma from himself.

After the memorial service ends, classes are canceled for the day, and Jake makes for the door. He has to get out of here. Stat. He can't stop thinking about last night, about what happened to Duncan. Still, there's one thing he wants to check out. He darts out of the chapel and hurries over to Xavier Hall.

The building is empty and cool. The only sound comes from Jake's tennis shoes squeaking against the tile floors. He rushes to the end of the hall and starts taking the stairs to the basement. Within the first few steps the fluorescent light overhead flickers and goes out.

It's dark except for the red glowing letters of the EXIT sign.

Jake continues more slowly now, holding onto the handrail and feeling his way to the basement—the basement that has the geology lab where Duncan spent every lunch period, where he recently showed Jake a piece of sand that had turned into glass. He's not exactly sure why he wants to see the lab again. Maybe it's because he couldn't feel any connection with Duncan at the memorial service. Or maybe it just seems like the best place to say good-bye. It's a place where Duncan was happy.

The lab is at the midpoint of the hall, and someone has left the door open and the lights on. *That's strange,* Jake thinks. He takes a few more steps toward the lab. The carpet muffles the sound of his footsteps.

As soon as he gets to the door, he turns. His legs stiffen. He has to blink several times to convince himself that his eyes aren't playing tricks on him. Even then he's still not sure.

It's Duncan Boyce. Right there. Sitting on one of those black granite tables and studying a rock in his palm. His white dress shirt is smeared with black soot, and something about his face seems different.

"Duncan?" Jake asks as he stands frozen in the doorway, one hand gripping each side of the frame.

Duncan continues to concentrate on the rock. His legs dangle over the edge of the table.

"Duncan . . . is that you?"

He looks up at Jake. His face is red and blistery, and his left eye is missing. He closes his fist around the rock. Jake feels his stomach drop to his knees, and he can barely hear over the sound of his smashing heart.

"I have something for you," he says, and his voice reminds Jake of a car driving over gravel. Duncan reaches into his shirt pocket and pulls out something that rattles. He tosses it to Jake, who instinctively catches it with his right hand.

A box of matches.

"You're going to need those." Duncan laughs as soon as he says this. His teeth are black as coal.

Jake runs, scrambling toward the darkened staircase. He can still hear Duncan's laugh even as he takes the steps two at a time to get back to the first floor. *He's not real,* Jake keeps telling himself. *No way!*

As he climbs the last two steps, Jake trips. His body falls hard, and the side of his face slams into the floor. Right away it stings as if someone just slapped him.

He looks back at the staircase in a panic, breathing heavily and waiting to see if Duncan is following him.

Nothing . . .

Everything is still for a few moments. Jake exhales with relief. Then he hears the sound.

A steady tapping . . . It's getting louder.

Footsteps!

Jake's body still aches from the fall, but he gets to his feet fast.

"Are you all right?" a voice asks from behind him. Jake turns, startled. Emma and Lily are standing right behind him.

"Yeah," Jake replies, still somewhat out of breath. He glances at the empty staircase again, and the light flashes on. His body starts to shake nervously. "I just fell," he says, not wanting to mention Duncan. Not wanting to believe his eyes.

"What's in your hand?" Emma asks, looking at Jake's tightly clenched fist.

"I . . ." Jake didn't realize that he is still holding the box of matches that Duncan threw him.

He's afraid to look. How can he explain the matches to anyone, including himself? He inhales and opens his hand. Slowly. His fingers unfold like the skin of a peeled banana.

It's empty. But how? Jake could have sworn that he felt the box in his sweaty palm, that it was real.

"Come on," Emma says. She reaches for his open hand, and her skin feels cool and soft. "Let's get out of here."

With that, Jake lets Emma and Lily lead him out of the building. He is still anxious about his dream of Emma, but he's relieved to get as far away from Duncan's ghost as possible. He wants to say something about it to Emma but can't—not with Lily there. One look at her bloodshot eyes and curved shoulders makes him realize that she can hardly hold up under the grief she's carrying. Another word about Duncan might make the load too heavy.

They walk outside slowly, Jake in between the girls. Emma is leading them to the parking lot.

"Where are we going anyway?" he asks, still noticing the way her fingers feel interlaced with his.

Emma glances at Lily.

"To see a fortune-teller about a witch."

20

TALKING TO THE DEAD

Emma figures that Ms. Dupré will be at Mystic Dreams by now, so from school they walk several blocks to Main Street. Leaves cover the streets, and they swoosh and crackle loudly with each step.

Everyone is quiet. They're all tired, but with Lily it's different. She hasn't looked exhausted until today. Maybe it's not exhaustion, Emma thinks. Maybe it's a broken heart.

Or both.

None of them mentions Duncan or the fire. It's probably better that way. Emma can't imagine words helping any. *Sorry. Shocking. Unfair. Tragic.* She heard these and others like them throughout the service, but she knows that real pain is beyond words.

When they get to the purple-blue building of Mystic Dreams, Jake opens the door, and they hurry inside. The place is cool and quiet. The only sound comes from the trickling water of the meditation fountains. Once again, Mr. Offutt isn't there, and the usual sign sits on the front counter:

READINGS BY MADEMOISELLE DUPRÉ

IN BACK ⟶

Jake leads the way, walking into a narrow passageway and pushing through a curtain of colored beads.

Emma has never been back here. It's smaller and plainer than she expected. Bland wallpaper. A cracked mirror. A few dreamcatchers with price tags on them hanging from the ceiling. It doesn't seem like a place where fortunes and magic are possible.

Ms. Dupré sits behind a small desk, wearing a red gown and studying several tarot cards spread in front of her. Stacks of books have been piled against each wall, making the room feel smaller than it already is. A thick aroma of incense permeates everything.

"I told you about that boy," Ms. Dupré says, not looking up from the cards.

"We need to ask you about Terrence Mallory," Emma begins tentatively. "Terry."

Ms. Dupré collects the cards in her hands and restacks the deck. "The boy's trouble," she mutters, but Emma isn't sure if she means Jake or Terry.

"We need your help," Emma pleads. "Please."

Ms. Dupré looks up, gazing at Jake with narrow eyes. "If you have questions, get to asking 'em, then."

"Has Terry ever come to you about casting spells?"

"Spells?"

"Yeah . . . like for causing people to sleepwalk."

Ms. Dupré smiles. "Sure, he's bought a few books and some ingredients for things, but that boy couldn't cast a fishing line without hooking himself."

"But if he has all of the things he needs—"

"You don't learn real magic from books you buy on the Internet and in a place like this." Ms. Dupré folds her hands and leans forward. "You got to live magic. It has to be taught, to be passed on. Besides, the last thing he'd want to do is make folks walk in their sleep."

"Why do you say that?"

"He's just like y'all. He hasn't slept in days."

Emma's face feels warm as if she has just been in the sun a long time, and her legs shake. She puts her hands on the back of the chair across from Ms. Dupré for support. "Terry can't sleep either?"

"That's right. Now, you need to get on your way. I have a client coming soon and—"

"This is bullshit!" Jake blurts. "All of it!" He glances around the room and then looks down at her cards. "You sit here and say bad things are happening like we don't know that. But who's doing this to us?"

Ms. Dupré shakes her head.

"Of course." Jake spits out the words. "You have no idea, and you aren't doing anything about it—except sitting here with those stupid cards and watching us die!"

No one speaks for a few moments. Emma can hear the faint sound of a ticking clock, but she doesn't see one in the room.

Ms. Dupré stands, and her body seems enormous in the smallness of the room. "My sister almost drowned once, and after that she could talk to the dead like we're talking now. Talking to the dead could never bring them back, though. It's like . . ." Ms. Dupré turns toward one of the bookcases. "You see those books over there? Some of them was saved from Katrina. They're all moldy and warped from the floods, but I wouldn't leave without them. No. I dragged 'em all the way up here. They were my mama's and her mama's before that. Books about spells and magic and believing in things you can't see. It's strange what you cling to when the world is coming to an end."

She looks at Emma and Jake and Lily. Her face appears lined and much older now. "Nothing could have stopped that hurricane. Dead bodies from cemeteries, friends and neighbors who drowned—all floating in the streets. Houses and roads wiped away so fast you couldn't believe your eyes. Some things just can't be stopped. All you do is learn to accept it." Ms. Dupré exhales audibly, and her big body seems to get smaller. "Have you been dreaming of her?" Ms. Dupré asks, glancing at Jake. "Is it drowning this time or something else?"

Jake's mouth drops, and he gets white as a sheet.

"So you haven't told her yet." Ms. Dupré's mouth opens partway into a smile. "You come here for answers, but what can I say that you don't already know? The fear, the guilt, the secrets, the bad things you've seen and done—they're inside of you, yes. But pulling your body from sleep to act out violence . . . well, that can come from outside. From somewhere else."

"How?" Jake asks, his voice tight.

"It could be nothing more than the sound of someone's voice," Ms. Dupré explains.

"Like hypnosis?" Emma asks, remembering the books on mesmerism that Dr. Beecher gave Duncan.

Ms. Dupré nods. "It's possible. It doesn't take much to unleash the dark and ugly things inside of us. Now it's time for you to go." She glances at the cards on her desk. "I have things to attend to."

Jake still seems stunned as Emma reaches for his hand and

starts pulling him toward the beaded curtain. He feels heavy as a sack of wet flour. But Lily isn't moving either. She has been standing in the same spot since they stepped into Ms. Dupré's office.

"Ms. Dupré?" The words squeak out of Lily's mouth.

"Yes."

"Can you speak to the dead . . . like your sister?"

Ms. Dupré's body seems to loosen, and her voice gets soft as a feather against your skin. "No, child. But you can say goodbye to someone even after he's gone. You just have to find a way that's right for you."

With that, Ms. Dupré ushers them out of her office. The front of the store is still empty as they pass the counter and step outside. Jake looks pale and unsteady. Lily sniffles quietly.

"Hypnosis," Emma mutters, but she's not sure to whom.

"What?" Jake asks as he lets go of her and shoves his hands into the front pockets of his black jeans.

"Duncan was talking to Dr. Beecher about it the night he died. And that lighter . . . It's like what Oristine did to you."

Lily's body stiffens, and she clasps her hands in front of her. "What are you saying?"

"I'm saying that Dr. Beecher has the knowledge. He saw what happened in New Orleans. At school and at his house, he keeps showing us—"

Emma stops herself, and the image of Lazarus being unearthed from the grave sends a chill down her spine.

"The paintings," she adds. The flashing white lights. The violent images. "What if he's using the paintings to do it?"

"Wait a minute," Jake says, looking between Lily and Emma. "How would that be possible?"

"I'm not sure. But it's something we've all been exposed to."

"Yeah, but—," Jake begins.

"It's worth checking out, at least." Emma glances at her watch. "I think we should wait until it gets dark and sneak into school. It'll be easier to look at the slides there than at Dr. Beecher's place."

"But that doesn't explain why," Lily says defensively. "Why would he want to hurt us? We're his favorite students."

Emma shakes her head, and then something comes to her. "Remember that stuff he said about his former students? About how they've disappointed him? Maybe he sees us the same way now. Maybe he doesn't trust us to keep quiet about New Orleans anymore."

The words make Emma's legs feel weak, and everyone gets quiet. She hadn't thought about that possibility until now. Still, the idea of Dr. Beecher causing their nightmares seems both possible and impossible at the same time. Maybe she's so desperate for an answer that she'll blame Dr. Beecher or anyone else right now.

"So what do we do until then?" Lily asks, her body still rigid.

"A Starbucks run." Emma tries to smile but can't.

"I . . ." Jake hesitates. "I'm not sure I should be around you right now. It's not safe."

The words send a pain through her chest. He has felt so far away since the night they slept together, yet all she can think about is being with him again. Maybe that night made him realize that he doesn't want her after all.

"Why?" Emma asks.

"Ms. Dupré was right," he admits. "I dreamed about you last night. We were in Dr. Beecher's house. I—" He lowers his eyes.

"Go on," Emma says.

Jake takes a step back. "You were lying on the living room floor. Bleeding from your ear. I saw you there, and . . . I should go. It can't be—"

"It doesn't matter what you saw," Emma interrupts. "We all just need to stick together. We have to help each other stay awake today—until we figure out what Dr. Beecher's role is in all this. Come on, Jake." Emma's voice softens. "We need to stay together. I need you."

Jake nods. "I need you, too."

21
THE DEATH OF SARDANAPALUS

Breaking into your high school at night isn't as hard as you might think, Jake realizes. He knows not to go for the doors: They're sure to be locked and might even be wired with alarms. But windows in an old building like Xavier Hall . . . now that's a possibility. Narrow openings but big enough to squeeze through. And they're probably just latched.

Or so they hope.

As they crouch beneath one of the windows to Dr. Beecher's classroom, the rain falls harder, and Jake can feel the wetness soaking through his clothes. Emma opens her backpack quickly. Since her house is closer to school than Jake's, she insisted on grabbing some random tools there—several screwdrivers, two hammers, a small flashlight, one small crowbar, a drill with no bits, and a wrench.

"Are you planning to do some construction work?" Jake asks.

"Yeah, I thought we could put in a skylight to brighten up the place," Emma says. She looks into the open bag. "So what's our tool of choice?"

Jake reaches up to the window and pulls. It swings outward with ease. He faces Emma with a smile, and she rolls her eyes.

"I so knew that would happen."

Jake then laces his fingers together and offers his hands as a step to boost Emma up to the ledge. The bottom of her tennis shoe is thick with mud. She goes up and slips inside fast. Jake passes her the backpack. Lily is next. Once they're both inside, Jake grabs onto the sill and pulls himself up.

It feels good to be out of the rain. Jake wipes his muddy hands on his pants and watches the flashlight glow as Emma makes her way to the center of the room. Jake's eyes adjust to the dark, and the room looks like it always does. Four rows of desks, the chalkboards, the ancient projector in the center, Dr. Beecher's small, beat-up desk.

"What do we do now?" Lily whispers.

"Take a closer look, I guess," Emma says as she snaps on the projector.

It hums loudly, and then a painting appears on the screen. Chaotic. Violent. Men wearing turbans, naked women, and piles of gold and jewels surround a king. He lies comfortably on a bed with red covers, watching as the violence unfolds. A dead woman has fallen at his feet. In the foreground a man stabs a naked woman, while another man pulls at the reins of a terrified horse. To the sultan's left another man seems to be in the process of killing two more women. The red covers, which spill onto the floor, remind Jake of blood.

"Delacroix," Lily mutters, and her voice sounds far away. "Dr. Beecher said we were going to study his paintings this week. I think this is *The Death of Sardanapalus*—a king who ordered his servants to kill his animals and concubines before he set fire to himself and his palace."

To Jake this painting seems like a cruel joke. Lily shouldn't have to see it, he tells himself. Not now. Not after what happened to Duncan. Why would Dr. Beecher choose to show this one? Why would he do that to Lily? Maybe, he *is* manipulating them.

For the first time Jake thinks Emma might be right.

Jake turns to Emma, who doesn't seem to be listening to Lily. She has moved closer to the screen and stopped a few inches from the horse. Jake realizes that the animal is not merely terrified. It is being stabbed by the man pulling the reins.

"What?" Jake asks.

"Weird," Emma says, pointing to the arm of the man stabbing the horse. "It looks like a scratch or something. Here too." She traces her finger down the man's arm and then along the horse's bent leg. She makes the L-shaped motion again.

"Where?" Jake stands next to her as he asks this, and he can smell the fragrance of shampoo in her damp hair. Something with apples.

"There."

She points again, and he can just make out two lines. "It's probably a bad reproduction," he suggests.

"When has Dr. Beecher ever used a bad reproduction?"

"Fair enough."

Emma returns to the projector and struggles to remove the slide reel. The painting wobbles on the screen. "Help me with this."

Jake tries to pull off the circular carousel, but it seems locked in place. He lifts it slightly, then twists it again with more force. It snaps off with a loud crack, and something falls to the floor.

"Oops," Jake mutters.

Emma puts the flashlight on the projector cart and takes the carousel from Jake. After removing the top, she starts lifting out slides. One at a time, stacking them next to the flashlight. After about seven or eight she hands the reel back to Jake.

"I wonder if it'll show up better like this," Emma says as she shuffles the slides in front of the light. "Here it is."

She holds the slide above her head and grabs the flashlight. Jake leans in close as they look up at the miniature version of the Delacroix. His face is practically pressed against hers.

"I can't see the marks," Emma says.

She adjusts the angle of the flashlight several times but stops when the beam is almost directly below the image. The light catches the scratches now. White, rough lines that have stripped away the gold, red, and blue paints of the canvas. But the lines don't just form an L anymore. There are several more, spread across the painting.

"What is all that?" Jake whispers. Something about the dark and being so close to her makes him lower his voice.

"I think it's a word." Emma turns to him, her mouth partway open and her eyes wide. "Let's put the carousel back on."

Jake fastens the plastic cylinder back in place, though it doesn't sit on the projector as firmly as before. Emma drops the slide in and once again the painting appears on the screen.

She steps up close and traces her finger on the surface. "L . . . ," she says after moving down the servant's arm and across the horse. She then draws a line from the servant's elbow to his thigh.

"I . . ."

Now she points to the man killing the naked woman in

the foreground. Her finger starts at his knife, slides down the concubine's arm, and then cuts across the man's bended knee. "Another L," she says. "And Y."

She draws that letter from his shoulder to the gold piled in the corner.

"Lily," Emma recites. "Her name has been written onto the image somehow. . . . I can't believe it."

She turns around, waiting for Jake to say something, it seems, but he can't speak. A dull pain has started throbbing in his forehead, and he wonders if it's being caused by the painting. Or maybe it's just the idea that Dr. Beecher is really responsible for his nightmares and possibly all the terrible things that have been happening in town. Jake presses his fingers against his temples to relieve the pressure. It doesn't help much.

"Where *is* Lily?" Emma asks suddenly.

"What?"

Jake looks around the room and realizes that Lily is gone. Emma calls out to her a few times, but the rain is pounding so heavily against the building that the sound of it swallows most of her voice. She turns to Jake again.

"Where did she go?"

"I . . . ," he begins, with a heavy feeling in his stomach. "I think I know."

With that, Jake leads her into the dark hallway and toward the stairs to the basement. There's only one place she'd go, he figures. One place where she might see Duncan again.

It's damn cold downstairs, Jake thinks. The kind of cold that creeps up your body when your socks and shoes are wet. He can feel it as soon as they get to the bottom of the stairs. The entire basement smells moldy from the dampness. Jake and Emma walk alongside each other, and her flashlight bounces off the dull gray lockers. Partway down the corridor the door to the geology lab is open. Again. A faint light comes from inside.

As they get a little closer, Jake grabs Emma's arm.

"Wait," he whispers.

"What?"

He glances at the light coming from the lab and then looks at Emma. "Do you believe in ghosts?"

"Jesus Christ, Jake," she snaps. "Stop messing around."

She tries taking another step, but Jake doesn't let go of her. "I'm serious. I saw something yesterday. When I was down here."

Emma studies his face for a moment. "What?"

"I'm not sure exactly. I thought . . ." He lowers his eyes. "I thought I saw Duncan in the lab. All scarred and blistered from the fire."

"Jake," she says softly, "it was in your head. You just imagined it. We're all freaked out right now."

Without another word she leads him toward the door. Jake's legs feel rubbery, and there is a sour taste at the back of his throat. A few more steps and they reach the lab. From the doorway Jake scans the room. It's not bright like before. This time the only light comes from a bulb in the glass refrigerator in the corner. It gives off a yellow glow.

The lab appears to be empty, Jake notes with relief. Narrow black tables. Wooden stools. A poster of the periodic table of elements taped against the back wall. Then he sees something out of place. A shape . . . a body. Someone sitting on the table farthest from the door.

Jake inhales sharply. This isn't where Duncan sat last time. He was on the first table, and every detail was clear from the lights overhead: the clothes, the texture of his burnt skin, the blood-red and blackened skin where his eye should have been.

"Lil," Emma calls out.

There's no answer, just a staccato sound. Staggered breathing. Emma points her flashlight at the body. The long hair, the slumped shoulders. Jake is pretty sure it's Lily. They move closer. Somehow Emma's flashlight makes everything away from the beam seem darker.

Lily covers her face as she sobs.

"It's okay," Emma says, touching her shoulder.

Jake half expects to see Duncan behind those hands, but then he hears Lily's voice. He's relieved that she is here. That she's alive.

"Come on." Emma's voice is quiet, and without saying a word Lily slides off the counter and lets herself be led to the door.

Jake glances around the room one more time, wondering if he really did see Duncan that time or if it was just his imagination after all.

"Jake?" Emma asks, turning toward him. "Is everything okay?"

He exhales. "Yeah . . . Let's get the hell out of here."

22
RED DOOR

Emma walks upstairs from the school basement with Lily and Jake, but when they get back into the classroom, Emma isn't sure what to do. She wants to go through all the slides—to see which ones have their names. Emma. Jake. Duncan. Susann. But Dr. Beecher keeps dozens of boxes filled with hundreds of slides on the shelves by his desk. It would take hours to go through them.

Emma checks her phone.

"Still nothing from Caitlin," she says. They've been calling her all afternoon, but she hasn't answered. "If she's at Dr. Beecher's place right now, we have to get her out of there."

"How are we going to do that?" Jake asks, standing next to the open window and looking outside anxiously.

"We've got to confront Dr. Beecher. We have to find out if all this is true—"

"You think he's just going to admit it?" Jake snaps. "We're totally screwed here. There's no way the cops will believe us."

Emma picks up the slide of Delacroix's *The Death of Sardanapalus.* "We have this."

"That doesn't prove anything."

"It's a start," Emma replies as she puts the slide into her pocket. "Maybe it's enough to make Dr. Beecher nervous."

"Nervous about what? All he has to do is wait until we fall asleep and kill each other!"

The words hit Emma like a slap. *He's right,* she thinks. *It's not safe to fall asleep.* Not before figuring out a way to undo the effects of the hypnosis.

"I'm sorry," Lily blurts out. She looks at Jake and Emma nervously, clasping her hands in front of her. "I . . . I can't deal with this right now. I have to go."

"What?" Emma begins, but Lily is already backing into the hall. "Wait a minute—"

"Sorry," she mutters again. "I just can't."

Emma starts to follow her, but she knows it's no good. Lily is already hurrying down the corridor, her arms swinging by her sides. Crying. Then she pushes open the double doors leading outside. No alarm sounds after all. Instead, it is just quiet.

Emma understands. Lily's heart has already been wrung dry, squeezed into a narrow, twisted thing. She can hardly believe that Duncan is gone, and now to think that Dr. Beecher is responsible . . . it's too much. Maybe it's too much for all of them, Emma considers.

She steps back into Dr. Beecher's classroom.

"I'm sorry I snapped," Jake says. "It's these damn headaches. . . . They started with the dreams."

"It's okay." Emma moves toward him and picks up her backpack. She wants him to touch her, but she knows he won't. Not right now. The fear, the exhaustion, the memories of New Orleans . . . it all keeps getting between them.

"If Dr. Beecher is causing this," she continues, "we have to stop him. Tonight."

Jake nods.

They hurry down the hall, opening the same double doors

that Lily used. The rain pounds heavily against the ground outside. As they leave, Emma glances back at Saint Opportuna. The tall brick buildings seem like fortresses, and the stone cross in the front yard reminds her of a scarecrow.

They start running toward Prospect Street. Fast. Emma is ahead of Jake at first, and every once in a while they stop under a tree to get out of the downpour. But the angry winds prevent them from getting dry.

Everything is wet. Her hair. Her clothes. Her shoes and socks. Even the streets are saturated with inches of water. Some of it rushes toward the gutters, while the rest puddles on the uneven cement.

"Come on," Emma says.

They begin running again. Emma can feel her muscles burn from the steep incline of the hill. Once they get to the top, they'll almost be there, she tells herself. The street will level off, and they'll be able to see the turrets of Dr. Beecher's yellow house. The trees on both sides of them shake violently from the wind. Emma reaches for Jake's hand as they continue up the hill together. Now she struggles to keep up with his long strides. The tools in her book bag slam hard against her back with each step.

When they get to the top, Emma and Jake turn onto Prospect.

In the late night sky Dr. Beecher's place makes her think of a haunted house. Sharp angles without color in the dark. Her stomach tightens as they approach the walkway. One color stands out here: the red door. It reminds her of the bedcovers in the Delacroix painting.

Red like the color of blood.

23

YEARBOOKS

Everyone freaks out once in a while, and Jake has had more than his fair share of times in the last week. Now that he's standing in the rain and staring at Dr. Beecher's porch, Jake can't seem to move his legs. It's just like his nightmare. The red door. The swing rocking back and forth in the wind.

That's what he can't tell Emma. He doesn't want to go inside. Not with her. Not to the place where he has dreamed of killing her.

"I don't think this is a good idea," he says.

Emma either doesn't hear, or she's just ignoring him. She lets go of his hand and jogs up the path. Jake follows. His clothes stick heavily to his body, and he can feel the water pooled in his tennis shoes, squishing between his toes.

The steps leading up to the porch creak under his feet, and he glances at the swing.

"Ready?" Emma asks.

"No."

She reaches for the doorknob, but Jake stops her. He takes a deep breath and places his palms on the door. It's dry. *It's not covered with blood,* he thinks with relief.

"What are you doing?"

"Nothing," he says, turning the handle and opening the unlocked door. "Let's do it."

Inside the foyer he can see a white light flashing in regular intervals from the living room—as if someone were turning a switch on and off. Water pours off Jake in steady streams, and a chill shakes his upper body. He peels off his soaking jacket before dropping it to the floor. Emma does the same, removing her backpack and then her coat.

The living room is empty. No candles burn on the circular table, but the projector hums loudly in the corner. With a loud click it flashes a white box onto the screen above the fireplace every few seconds, as if it is running through an empty carousel. Something about the clicking and bursts of white light make Jake's eyes feel heavy. All of a sudden a painting appears on the screen: *The Raising of Lazarus.*

Emma grabs Jake's hand. "Don't look!"

She pulls him back into the foyer, and he stumbles at first, surprised by how heavy his legs still feel. She leads him down a narrow hallway. His head is throbbing again, and the pain causes him to see white spots everywhere. He stops after a few steps and leans against the wall. His forearm feels tight.

"I can't," he mumbles.

Emma presses her cool hands against his face. It feels good having her touch him. He looks at her face. It's damp and shiny with rainwater.

"Yes, you can," she says. "His office is just down here."

They take a few more steps together and enter the room.

It's warm and stuffy. A faint light glows from the floor lamp in the corner, and an old frayed tapestry covers the wall where a window should be. Jake studies the bleeding knight and the raven for a moment. He wonders if this is another trick, like all the other paintings. The kind of thing to give them nightmares. He has a sudden urge to tear the damn thing off the wall.

Jake notices the papers and books scattered across a desk. There is also a stack of Saint Opportuna yearbooks there. One from 1999 has been left open, and a photograph of a student has a circle around it. Perhaps he was one of Dr. Beecher's students, Jake thinks. Like the lobbyist for big tobacco or the car thief. He's not sure, but the picture makes Jake wonder how many pages of how many yearbooks are filled with students who have disappointed Dr. Beecher. *Is that what disappointment turns into?* Jake wonders. *Anger? Is that why this is happening?*

Emma stands on the opposite side of the empty office, staring at a bookshelf. She turns toward Jake.

"Here are some books on mesmerism—," she says, then stops abruptly. Her mouth drops, and her eyes get wide. She's not looking at him, Jake realizes. She's looking over his shoulder. At something behind him. Jake spins around, but not fast enough.

His head explodes with a pain that's worse than all of his headaches combined. Everything goes black.

24
THE LAST PICTURE SHOW

Emma can't see who hits Jake. A shadow appears out of the darkness of the hallway, reaches inside the room, and strikes him on the back of the head. Then the shadow is gone. Jake's body falls to the floor with a loud crash.

Emma hurries over to him. She lifts up his head and starts running her fingers through his hair.

"Jake . . . Jake? Wake up!"

He groans but doesn't move. She continues to touch his hair—looking from him to the doorway, wondering if the shadow will come back. Her breathing is short and quick. Then she feels something sticky by Jake's left ear. She pulls her hand away. Blood covers her fingertips.

Thud.

The sound comes from somewhere in the front of the house. *I've got to do something,* Emma tells herself. She reaches for her cell to call the police, but the phone isn't in her pocket. *Crap.*

She must have slipped it into her coat. The coat she left by the front door. Emma checks Jake's pockets next, but his phone isn't there either. She scans the room for a land line. Nothing—just books and antique furniture. She wonders where Dr. Beecher is. Why did he hit Jake and leave? Did he expect them to come? Is that why the projector is running in the front room?

She looks down at Jake again. "I'll be back," she whispers.

She steps around Jake and enters the hall. At the far end, in the foyer she sees flashes of light coming from the living room, but they're no longer white. Each one is filtered with color. The projector must be running through slides, she thinks.

Emma creeps forward, staying close to the wall. Her shoes squeak on the hardwood floor, and the sound seems to be synchronized with the clicking projector. She takes a few more quick steps. Now, she's close enough to see the vine-carved handrail of the staircase. Its intricate design shifts and changes in the blinking, colored light. She pauses, trying to steel herself before passing the entrance to the living room.

She peers into the room but doesn't see anyone. *Where is he?* The chairs and couch are empty. On the screen above the fireplace another image—Rembrandt's *The Blinding of Samson*—appears over and over again, as if the machine were stuck in some kind of groove. The knife buried in Samson's eye. The men holding him on the floor. And Delilah fleeing the tent with the scissors in her hand. All of these images make Emma's eyes feel heavy.

Stop looking! she tells herself.

She goes back to the foyer. Her coat and backpack are gone. Jake's, too. Only pools of rainwater remain, and she stares at them in disbelief. She doesn't know what to do next. She's afraid to leave Jake behind. She can't do that. Then she remembers the call Dr. Beecher took about Jeremy's death. He answered it in front of them.

In the living room!

Emma hurries inside again and goes toward the corner where Dr. Beecher answered the phone. She remembers it being on a small table next to a lamp that was never turned on. Neither the table nor the lamp is there. Instead she finds a rack with overcoats and umbrellas. The alternating light and dark from the projector make it difficult for Emma's vision to adjust, and she wonders if her eyes are playing tricks on her. She frantically pushes aside the coats, trying to find the phone on the floor.

Nothing. Just the smell of mothballs.

Behind her the floor creaks suddenly. Emma spins around, but only has time to see a fireplace poker swinging at her head. She ducks. The heavy shaft shatters the coat rack, and umbrellas spill onto the floor. Emma scrambles toward the middle of the room, keeping her head lowered. She looks back, but the room is dark again.

She hears a grunt, and then the poker slams into her shoulder, knocking her into one of the chairs by the coffee table. Her left arm throbs and tingles from the blow. She grabs the back of the wooden chair and tosses it wildly at the person in the shadows. It misses but puts some distance between them.

The painting flashes on the screen again, and in the light Emma can see Caitlin's face. Teeth bared. The muscles of her neck taut. She lunges at Emma with the poker, driving the sharp end into her stomach.

Emma stumbles back against the fireplace. She struggles to breathe, and her stomach burns from where it cut into her skin.

Caitlin raises the poker over her shoulder and takes another step.

"Stop!" Emma yells.

Caitlin hesitates. Samson projects onto the screen, and Caitlin's white skin appears stained with spots of brown, black, and dark blue. Her eyes have become as dark as the canvas.

"You're not who you think you are!" Emma pleads. "It's the paintings. Dr. Beecher has been using them to control us."

"Dr. Beecher . . . ," Caitlin says.

"Yes. He has been manipulating the slides." Emma pulls the slide out of her pocket. "We found this in his classroom. It has Lily's name inscribed on it—"

Caitlin swings the poker again. This time it strikes Emma's arm. She can feel her head hit the coffee table as she falls, and she rolls onto the floor. Her left ear buzzes violently. She looks up at Caitlin, who is standing above her. The projector flashes on and off again, and everything in the room spins out of focus. Emma covers her left ear.

"Silas can't even work the projector!" Caitlin snaps. "Let alone adjust the slides."

Emma uses her right arm to prop herself up on her side. "Listen to me," she says, dragging herself away from Caitlin. "He's doing this to you. He's hypnotizing us. Like Oristine—"

"Don't be such an idiot, Emma!" Caitlin steps forward. "Imagine it—having the power to control the people around you, to make them do anything you want. What would you do?"

"What the hell are you talking about?" Emma asks, getting to her feet cautiously. Her ear still rings painfully, and the room wobbles like an out-of-focus film. The slide is still in her hand.

Caitlin doesn't speak for a moment, and her face is once again covered in the colored spots of the painting. She tightens her grip on the poker. "You could revenge your daughter's death, like Oristine. Or you could get rid of anyone you wanted—as long as your secret was safe."

"*You*?" Emma asks. She can feel blood trickling from her ear, and the side of her face burns. "You changed the slides?"

Caitlin smiles as if she just thought of something funny. "It started out simple. I wanted to show Silas how much better things would be around here without them. Jocks and cheerleaders and theater losers. Hell, there wasn't a brain cell among them. They couldn't appreciate art or culture. Not like me and Silas—"

"But . . . ," Emma begins without being sure what to say. "Where is he? Dr. Beecher?"

"Upstairs. I figured you'd come tonight, so I slipped him some sleeping pills. He'll be out for a while."

Emma can't think straight with her head pounding. But not all of the pain is coming from her injury. She can feel her anger at Caitlin growing, bubbling up inside. The projector continues to flash, and Emma retreats another step.

"Susann . . . ," Emma mutters. "She wasn't some goddamn cliché who couldn't think for herself! And what about Duncan? How could you do that to him? He was your friend. We're all—"

"My friends?" she asks mockingly. "Bullshit! I was never one of you."

"Whose fault is that?"

Caitlin shakes her head. "Like I said," she continues with forced calmness, "it started out simple. I wasn't sure what would happen, but once Susann and the others started sleepwalking, I knew the rest of you would trace it back to New Orleans. Don't you see? You're the only ones who could ruin it. You'd figure out I was responsible eventually. Then Duncan started reading about hypnosis. . . ." Caitlin moves forward slightly. "Well, I couldn't risk that. Besides, Silas is the only person I care about, and he's the only one who really cares about me."

Caitlin swings the poker. Emma jumps to the side, but it still catches her knee, dropping her to the floor. She cries out. This pain is different from before. It screams up and down her leg. Something is seriously wrong, Emma realizes. She tries touching her kneecap, but it hurts too much.

"He loves me," Caitlin hisses. "He doesn't need the rest of you. Can't you understand that?"

Emma tries to get off the floor now, but the pain in her knee is paralyzing. She glances behind her at the foyer. She realizes she can't even crawl that far at this point.

Suddenly, a sound comes from above her. Someone is walking down the staircase. Unsteadily. She sees slippers. A long midnight-blue robe. It's Dr. Beecher. He grips the vine-carved handrail with each heavy step, leaning his weight on it.

"What's going on here?" he asks groggily.

As soon as Dr. Beecher sees Emma, his mouth drops. He rushes down the rest of the stairs and approaches her—still shaken and unbalanced. He tightens the robe around his waist.

"Uh . . . it's not what it looks like. I . . . we were—" He cuts himself off. "What happened to your face?"

"Silas," Caitlin calls out.

He turns toward her quickly. "Did you tell her about us?" His words are cold and sharp. Emma has never heard his voice that way. Even Caitlin recoils. "*Did you*?"

"She killed Duncan and Jeremy," Emma blurts out. "She's using your paintings to do it."

Dr. Beecher's eyebrows wrinkle as he looks down at Emma. "We need to get you to a doctor. Can you stand?"

Emma shakes her head. "You're not listening to me. It's just like what Oristine did in New Orleans. I can prove it. I brought a slide from class. It has Lily's name drawn into it. Caitlin was going to hypnotize her next."

"Shut up!" Caitlin yells.

Dr. Beecher shakes his head and exhales loudly. "What are you talking about?"

"The paintings that you show us over and over again. They've been altered," Emma says. "I think it has to do with the repeated exposure and the white lights. I don't know how. But I'm pretty sure Duncan read about that kind of thing in your books."

"That's not possible," Dr. Beecher replies.

"Look at the slide!"

Emma hands it to him. He takes it reluctantly and holds it up to the light. He squints as he brings it close to his face.

"It looks damaged, that's all. . . ." He rotates the slide back and forth a few times before lifting it high above his head. Then the expression on his face starts to change. His features tighten, and his arm gets still. He turns to Caitlin. "Have you been manipulating these?"

She shifts her weight from one foot to the other nervously. "You talk about it all the time. No one seeing beneath the surface of things. A generation of students who don't read, who are closed off, who communicate in fifteen-character sentences instead of talking to each other. 'Doesn't the world deserve better?' That's what you said just the other night!"

Caitlin glares at him, and tears start streaming down her face.

"I was upset. I'd just found out about my former students and—" Dr. Beecher stops. His voice softens. "What have you done?"

"I'm trying to show everyone that you're right!" Caitlin snaps, and her face appears distorted from the colors of the painting. "What I saw Oristine do to Jake and Selene . . . She could change things. But that's not all. 'Hypnosis requires a willingness on the part of the subject to submit himself to visual or auditory cues.' That's what one of your books said. It happens every day, just like you said. People sitting in front of computers and televisions—taking in images all the time and not realizing how it changes them, how it makes them less human. I wanted to see how easily they could be manipulated. To see how quickly they'd turn on each other."

"I don't understand," Dr. Beecher says. "You were able to make them *kill*?"

"Not exactly. I don't know how to direct someone to do something. Not like Oristine did. The hypnosis seems to unleash something terrible, something violent inside them.

Something already there." Caitlin pauses, struggling with the words. "At first I just wanted to see what they would do. I didn't think . . ."

"What the hell is wrong with you?" Dr. Beecher's face turns red.

"The world deserves better, Silas. Now you know for sure. I mean . . . you can forget about them. You can have me instead."

Dr. Beecher opens his mouth, but no words come out. He stares at her as if she were a ghost. "Give me the poker," he says sternly, holding out his hands. "Come on. We have to get Emma to a hospital."

"What?"

"The poker."

"No, you're not helping her." Caitlin steps back and lifts the poker again. Her face tightens and then falls slightly, as if she doesn't recognize Dr. Beecher, as if she realizes for the first time that he's not the person she thought he was. "Get out of the way."

"What are you—"

"Move!"

Caitlin glares at Emma. All the fury and rage have rushed back into her face. Dr. Beecher sees her expression change and steps in between her and Emma.

"You're not going to hurt her," he says, with the same booming authority he uses in class. "I want you to give me the poker. Okay?"

"Okay."

With that she shoves the pointed end of it into his groin.

Dr. Beecher coughs loudly as the air explodes from his mouth. He bends over with his hands between his legs.

Caitlin faces Emma again and raises it above her head. Emma, her heart pounding and body screaming in pain, can't think of anything else to do but close her eyes.

25

PARASOMNIA

He drags his hands along the walls of the dark narrow corridor. The rough, uneven surface feels as if it's encoded with a message—like Braille. It's moist, too. Something oozes from the walls.

A light flashes at the far end of the hall.

On . . . off.

On . . . off.

It draws him forward, pulling him. His feet move with the rhythm of its regular clicking sound. He wants to collapse on the floor and curl into a tiny ball. But his feet keep marching ahead. A tightness seizes his hand. He looks down and realizes that he's gripping something narrow and sharp.

A letter opener. He must have taken it from Dr. Beecher's desk.

He is almost at the light now. He can see the vines of a wood-carved staircase. And then her body on the ground, blood smeared on her face. The birthmark. Her eyes are closed.

Someone is bent over her . . . or is he seeing himself perched above her body? Moments away from plunging the letter opener into her.

No, it has to be someone else—someone who wants to hurt her.

He can't let that happen. He has to do something.

The light snaps off again.

He charges forward—

26
BROKEN THINGS

Emma opens her eyes just as Jake stumbles into the room. It's as if he has lost his balance and is about to fall over. Instead he keeps moving—staying on his feet until he collides with Dr. Beecher. They hold each other for a few seconds like two exhausted boxers in a ring. Then Jake steps back abruptly, shaking his head.

"No," he cries out. He looks at his hand and studies the letter opener, as if he's not sure what it is or how it got there.

"Look at the screen, Jake," Caitlin says. Her voice hums steadily. "Look at the screen, and don't take your eyes off it."

Jake turns toward Rembrandt's *The Raising of Lazarus* on the wall above the fireplace. The projector clicks, and the image is replaced by a white square. Emma watches as well, though she tries to stop. She wants to yell out to Jake, to tell him to look away, but she can't speak. Her eyes feel heavy. There is another click, and Lazarus's ghostly body reappears.

"She's on the floor, Jake," Caitlin continues, staring at Emma now. "You know what to do."

Jake faces Emma, his hands at his sides. The letter opener is aimed directly at her.

"You know what to do," Caitlin repeats.

Jake shakes his head again.

"*Now*," she hisses.

Suddenly, he lifts up his hand. Emma tries to slide away. If she can get into the hallway again—where it's dark, where Jake can't see the paintings—she'll be okay, she tells herself. She tries to move, but the pain shoots up her leg. Paralyzing. Jake takes a step. The projector clicks again as he towers over her. His face is lost in the shadows of the dark room.

Then he relaxes his arms.

"No," he says, turning toward Caitlin. "I won't. You can't make me."

Caitlin presses her lips together angrily and looks at Dr. Beecher, who has been watching everything with a mixture of shock and pain on his face. He is standing now. One hand still covers his groin. Caitlin's mouth hangs partway open, as if she expects Dr. Beecher to do something.

"Enough," Jake says. "It's over."

Suddenly, she drops the poker and reaches for his hand with the letter opener. Jake struggles to hold on. He pulls away, and they both stumble into the foyer.

Jake's head slams against the railing of the staircase, and Caitlin pulls free.

She spins around toward Emma again but doesn't see Dr. Beecher moving toward her now.

Emma can't see everything that happens next. There is a hollow, slapping sound, and Dr. Beecher gasps. Caitlin's hand is covered with blood. Then she thrusts the letter opener into him again.

And again.

Dr. Beecher's body shudders. He collapses onto the floor and presses his hands against the hole beneath his heart. A gurgling sound comes from his mouth. Bright, red blood spills onto his chest and the floor. His robe has fallen open, exposing his white, hairless legs.

Caitlin's eyes widen with surprise, and she drops to her knees beside him. "Silas," she cries, stroking his face.

Emma hears the projector click again, and she glances at the body of Lazarus on the screen. Despite the burning in her leg and on her face, she feels exhausted. Her eyes sting with tiredness, and it's difficult to keep them open. Dr. Beecher moans, and she can hear a whistling sound with each breath.

The room gets dark . . .

The doctor treating Emma smells like garlic and anchovy pizza. She knows this because she hates the smell of anchovies. Her dad likes them and usually makes her and Gwen go half and half when they order a pizza. Right now the aroma makes her stomach turn, and she tries to hold her breath. The doctor has deep brown eyes and dark circles underneath each. He looks as tired as she feels, Emma thinks.

He clears his throat before speaking. "*A-hem* . . . you have a mild concussion, so we're going to keep you for the rest of the night. Just as a precaution. Your father is on the way. I told him about your dislocated kneecap as well—"

"Um . . ." Emma tries to sit up, but the room starts spinning. Her leg burns. She sinks back into the bed. "What about Dr. Beecher?"

"He didn't make it. I'm sorry."

Emma can't think of what to say. She can still hear the gurgling sounds from his throat and see the blood oozing from his chest.

The doctor checks his watch quickly. "In the morning a sleep specialist is going to see you too. Your father mentioned your recent experience with sleepwalking, so I think it's a good idea to have a consultation. Okay?"

The doctor leaves without waiting for an answer.

Emma scans the room but doesn't see her coat or backpack anywhere. She'd like to check her phone for a message from Jake. She wonders where he is. The paramedics wouldn't let him ride with her to the hospital. She doesn't remember who called the police or how long it took for them to arrive. At one point she remembers seeing them escort Caitlin to a police car. "I didn't mean to. Not him," she said over and over. "Not him."

Emma's eyes feel heavy once again, and she closes them. *Just for a minute,* she tells herself. *A minute and that's it. Just until Dad and Gwen get here . . .*

The hole by her feet is getting deeper.

The heaviness of the shovel makes the muscles in her arms ache as she drives it into the earth again. She has to find out what the howling sound wants, she tells herself. She takes a step back.

Crack.

Something has broken underneath her foot. She picks up the glasses with their thick black frames and tosses them aside.

She continues digging. Soon the sky shifts from coal black to deep blue, and a light drizzle falls from the clouds. She sticks the shovel into the ground again and hits something. It's not hard, exactly, but it's too thick to penetrate. She pauses. Warm sweat covers her face and neck.

She reaches down and starts brushing away the dirt with both hands. The moist earth sticks to her hands. The ground is smooth in places. She clears aside more of it, and she can start to see a face. Long hair. Eyes wide open and the color of eggshell.

It's a face that looks naked without glasses.

Lily.

Emma wakes up in the hospital bed, out of breath and with sweat sticking to her forehead. The sheets have been kicked to the floor, and she is wearing her clothes from last night: dark jeans and a black T-shirt. They still feel damp. Her shoes have left clumps of dried mud on the bed.

What happened? When did I put my clothes back on?

She can picture Lily's face in the ground, pale white and smeared with dirt. Panic grips Emma. *Something must have happened to her,* Emma thinks. *Maybe I went looking for her in my sleep. Maybe—* Her head starts to spin, and the bandage wrapped around her left kneecap feels tight and hot. She looks around the room. The chair next to the bed is empty, but her father's reading glasses and a book are on the table there. He must have come and decided not to wake her up, she figures.

Right then Jake appears in the doorway.

"You're awake," he says with a smile, and he walks over to her. His black hair is disheveled, as if he just woke up.

"How long have I been asleep?" she asks.

"I don't know. I couldn't find where they were keeping you at first, and then I waited until I saw your dad and sister going down to the cafeteria." Jake glances at her clothes. "How are you feeling?"

Emma tries to sit up, but she feels dizzy. "Dr. Beecher's dead."

THOMAS FAHY

teaches literature at Long Island University's C. W. Post campus and lives in New York. He is the author of *The Unspoken*, his first book for teens, and *Night Visions*, a horror novel for adults. Visit him at thomasfahy.com.